"Don't you like us, Susan?"

His voice was low. "You've made it plain that you haven't much use for me, but surely Papa and Ben haven't offended you. Why are you punishing them?"

"Marc, you can't possibly believe that!" she sputtered indignantly. "Why, Papa Vito's the father I never had. I love the whole crazy Donatello family."

"And me?" Marc asked. "Where do I fit in? What am I to you?"

Susan was silent for a moment. "Try as I may, I can't fit you into any category. Certainly not brother. I'm not even sure that you want to be my friend. Part of the time you're mad at me, and at other times you're indifferent."

With a low groan Marc pulled her up on his lap and cradled her against him in an embrace that nearly squeezed the breath out of her. "I'm never indifferent to you, *cara*. You spend most of your time fending off my advances. You have me in such a state that I've either got to yell at you or make love to you."

Dear Reader,

Welcome to Silhouette. Experience the magic of the wonderful world where two people fall in love. Meet heroines who will make you cheer for their happiness, and heroes (be they the boy next door or a handsome, mysterious stranger) who will win your heart. Silhouette Romances reflect the magic of love—sweeping you away with books that will make you laugh and cry, heartwarming, poignant stories that will move you time and time again.

In the next few months, we're publishing romances by many of your all-time favorites, such as Diana Palmer, Brittany Young, Emilie Richards and Arlene James. Your response to these authors and other authors of Silhouette Romances has served as a touchstone for us, and we're pleased to bring you more books with Silhouette's distinctive medley of charm, wit and—above all—*romance*.

I hope you enjoy this book and the many stories to come. Experience the magic!

Sincerely,

Tara Hughes
Senior Editor
Silhouette Books

PHYLLIS HALLDORSON
To Choose a Wife

Silhouette **Romance**

Published by Silhouette Books New York

America's Publisher of Contemporary Romance

SiLHOUETTE BOOKS
300 E. 42nd St., New York, N.Y. 10017

Copyright © 1987 by Phyllis Halldorson

ISBN: 0-373-08515-X

First Silhouette Books printing July 1987

America's Publisher of Contemporary Romance

Printed in the U.S.A.

Books by Phyllis Halldorson

Silhouette Romance

Temporary Bride #31
To Start Again #79
Mountain Melody #247
If Ever I Loved Again #282
Design for Two Hearts #367
Forgotten Love #395
Undercover Lover #456
To Choose A Wife #515

Silhouette Special Edition

My Heart's Undoing #290
The Showgirl and the Professor #368

PHYLLIS HALLDORSON,

like all her heroines, is as in love with her husband today as on the day they met. It is because she has known so much love in her own life that her characters seem to come alive as they, too, discover the joys of romance.

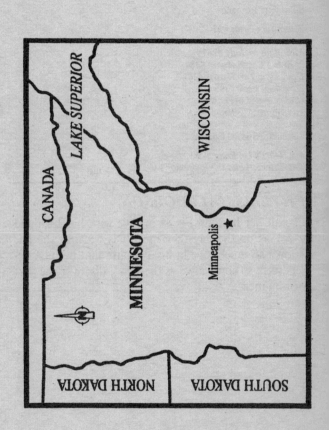

Chapter One

The red Ferrari hurtled down the highway at a speed far exceeding the legal limit, but to Marco Donatello, the tall, dark man behind the steering wheel, it seemed to be crawling. His foot pressed the gas pedal closer to the floor as his tumultuous thoughts sped ahead to the sprawling university hospital in Minneapolis.

Vito, Papa, Dad, the man who was known to Marco by all of those names, was a patient there, and he was going to die in the forseeable future!

Marco swore viciously. It had to be a grotesque practical joke that his brother, Benedetto, was playing on him. The telephone call that Ben had placed less than an hour before to tell him their father was in the hospital and had just been diagnosed as having leukemia must have been made when Ben was blind, staggering drunk and intent on a little horseplay with his elder brother.

But Ben seldom drank, and to Marco's knowledge, he'd never gotten drunk. He hadn't sounded smashed; he'd sounded shattered, and there was a big difference. Expertly Marc maneuvered the high-powered sports car in and out of traffic as it barreled toward its destination. It was early afternoon, and the traffic was reasonably light on this Wednesday in early July, but still it seemed as if he'd been driving for hours without making any progress. Like one of those time-warp dreams where you're in a panic to get somewhere, but your body moves only in slow motion. There was no immediate emergency, but it was important to Marc to be with his father as quickly as possible.

Leukemia. The ugly word hovered relentlessly in Marco's mind and refused to go away. How was it possible that Vito had developed a malignant blood disease? Marc couldn't remember his father ever being sick.

Vito was a big man, husky and strong. Even now, at age fifty-seven, his muscles were bulging and hard from his compulsive habit of shifting and rearranging heavy boxes of groceries during his almost daily visits to the warehouses of the twenty-five supermarkets that comprised the Donatello chain of Don's Markets in Minneapolis and St. Paul. His blood pressure hadn't varied in thirty years, and he'd only recently started wearing reading glasses.

Neither had he lost any of his virility, a fact to which at least two women could attest in the five years since his wife, Marc and Ben's mother, had died. Vito was a passionate man who had been true to his beloved Maria during the thirty years of their marriage, and for two years after her death. Then Sophia had come into his life, to be replaced later by Lisl.

Marco smiled. He never had figured out how blond, blue-eyed Lisl had managed to capture Papa's attention. He'd been born in Italy and was totally dedicated to his Italian heritage. He'd married an American girl of Italian parentage and insisted that their sons do likewise. Ben had, and Marc probably would when he decided to settle down to one woman and raise a family.

No, Sophia and Lisl may have warmed Vito's bed, but they'd never taken Maria's place in his heart.

Dammit all, there had to be some mistake. Papa couldn't die. He had at least thirty more years of life before him. *Nonno* Giovanni, Vito's father and founder of Don's Markets, had lived to be eighty.

It was after four o'clock when Marc pulled into the parking lot on the University of Minnesota campus and sprinted into the hospital.

He was met in the lobby by his brother, Benedetto, and Marc's first reaction was anger. "Just why in hell wasn't I told that Dad wasn't feeling well and had gone into the hospital for tests?" he demanded before he'd even said hello.

Ben ran his hand through his black curly hair. "Sorry, Marc, but that's the way he wanted it. I didn't even know about it until after he'd checked in here, and I work with him every day. You know how he is. He absolutely refused to let me call you until the results were in. Kept saying he was just tired and needed a few days rest. No reason to worry you."

"I was only in Duluth, for God's sake," Marc ranted, then took a deep breath in an effort to calm down. "Sorry," he said and gave his brother an affectionate clap on the shoulder. "I'd have done the same thing in your place. Neither of us ever got old enough or big enough to overrule Papa once he had his mind made up. So tell me what happened."

Ben managed a weak smile and put his arm around Marc's shoulders. "I will, but let's go get a cup of coffee first. You look like you could use something stronger, but they don't serve whiskey in hospitals."

They found the cafeteria, and took their mugs to a secluded table. "Now," Marc said, "start at the beginning and tell me what's going on."

Ben took a swallow of the hot black liquid. "So help me, I had no idea Papa wasn't well. He worked at least eight hours every day, made his usual rounds of the markets, kept tabs on the hiring and firing." He shrugged. "You know how he is. He makes it a point to know everything that's going on in each store."

Marc nodded. "Yeah, I know."

"Well, he apparently had a fainting spell on Sunday that I knew nothing about until later, so he went to see the doctor Monday morning. Leo Tornatori had him admitted here for tests, and I called you as soon as they got the results. Leo says there's no doubt about it, it's definitely leukemia."

Marc rubbed his hands over his face and slumped in the uncomfortable straight-backed chair. "He must have had symptoms before the episode on Sunday. Why didn't he say something or see the doctor sooner?"

Ben sighed. "You know Dad. He swears that he wasn't sick, just tired. Leo tells me he also admitted to a low-grade fever and pain in his joints, which he attributed to 'getting old.' Now that I really look at him, I can see that he's lost weight and he looks sort of—ravaged." He banged his fist on the table in frustration. "I should have noticed it earlier, but dammit, he seemed as energetic and vigorous as ever."

"Don't blame yourself, Ben," Marc said. "I should have been paying more attention, too. After I moved to Duluth in February to oversee the construction of the new market, I sort of lost track of what was going on here. This past month, what with pushing the contractor to get the building finished on time, and coordinating plans for the grand opening, it was easier to handle things by phone than make the trip back and forth. I hadn't realized until I got your call that I haven't seen Dad in well over a month."

The two men sipped their coffee in silence, each battling their private demons of guilt and sorrow. With a wrench Marc remembered that he'd spent the past weekend right here in Minneapolis with Hilary at her condo. He'd been so bemused with her strawberry-blond beauty that he hadn't even called Papa. If he had, he'd have known about the fainting spell and could have been with him these past few days.

He shook his head to dislodge his tormented thoughts and asked, "How's Dad taking this, Ben? Does he know how serious it is?"

"Oh hell, yes," Ben grated. "I was with him when Leo and the staff doctor gave him the news. I was too shocked to think straight, let alone ask questions, but Dad made them tell him everything they knew about the disease, and its prognosis. He seems to be taking it a whole lot better than we are, but he did ask for a priest. The hospital chaplain was with him when I came down here to wait for you, which was roughly an hour ago."

Marc was afraid to ask the next question. "What is the prognosis, Ben? How long does Papa have?"

Ben swallowed, and his black eyes shimmered with moisture. "The doctors wouldn't even make an educated guess, said there were too many variables. They're giving him a blood transfusion now, and if that perks him up, they'll send him home in a couple of days.

"Leo says there's a good chance that after the initial onset the disease will go into remission. If that happens, he'll be well enough to go back to work, and may live an almost normal life span. On the other hand, if it doesn't go into remission..." Ben chocked on a sob and didn't attempt to continue.

Marc felt the pain of pent-up tears in his own throat and clutched his brother's upper arm in sympathy as he pushed back his chair and stood. "I imagine the chaplain is finished with Dad by now. I want to see him. Do you think he's up to it?"

"He's been waiting for you," Ben said and stood also. "I'm going to take off. Carla will probably be home by the time I get there, and she doesn't know about this yet. I didn't see any reason to upset her at work with bad news when there's nothing she can do. She'll want to visit Dad as soon as possible, though, so we'll be back after dinner. See you then."

Marco stepped out of the elevator and followed the signs to the room number Ben had given him. He slowly pushed open the door, not wanting to wake Vito if he was asleep.

There were two beds, but one was empty. The other was partially elevated, and the familiar figure lying there was wearing a green hospital gown. A sheet and lightweight blanket covered him to the waist, and his eyes were closed.

Marco went in and shut the door carefully behind him, then tiptoed closer. Ben was right: Papa had lost weight, quite a bit of it, and there was a yellowish tinge under his swarthy complexion. His black hair and matching short beard were liberally sprinkled with

white, more so than Marc had remembered. He looked
older, vulnerable.

Marc blinked. Vulnerable? Papa? No way. He was
the rock, the foundation on which the family and the
business were built. He was the provider, the com-
forter, the one they'd all expected would fix things and
make them right.

Papa was indestructable.

A groan broke through Marc's restraint, and Vito
stirred and opened his eyes. He blinked and for a moment seemed to have difficulty focusing. Then his gaze
rested on Marc, and slowly he raised his arms and held
them out to his son. Marc leaned down into the embrace, and the two men hugged each other.

When they broke apart, Marco sat down on the side
of the bed, but it was Vito who spoke first. "Marco,
you should be in Duluth making sure the new market's
ready to open." His tone was gruff, but his face lit with
pleasure at seeing his firstborn son.

"Sure, Dad," Marc said with an attempt at lightness, "but I wanted to see you, so humor me." His
voice broke, and he reached into his pocket for his linen
handkerchief and blew his nose. A delaying tactic to
give him time to get himself under control.

"Ah, Marco," Vito said, "you've been listening to
Benedetto and those doctors. They say I'm going to die.
Well, so are they, and so are you. I just have a little
better idea of when it's going to happen to me than most
people do."

He patted Marc's leg. "That's not necessarily bad.
Now that I know what the problem is, I can fight it.
When your mother died, I prayed for God to take me,
too, but he didn't. Now I'm no longer willing to go. I
still have family to welcome."

Marc snapped to attention. "Family to welcome? What are you talking about? You, Ben and I are all that's left of our family. And Carla, of course," he amended, including Ben's wife.

"For now, yes," Vito agreed, "but I'm going to see you married, and hold your first *bambino* in my arms before I join Maria."

Marco's lack of a wife and children had been a source of contention between him and his father for years, and even now Marc felt a stab of resentment that he quickly banished. "Good," he said, "then you'll be around for a long time so you can get to know your grandchildren."

Vito sighed. "I intend to know my *nipote*, but I need some cooperation from you for that. It appears that I'm never going to get any from Benedetto."

"Dad, you know that's something Ben and Carla have no control over. They've always wanted a baby."

"I know, I know." Vito's disappointment was strong in his voice. "So, it's up to you. Are you going to marry Hilary Granville?"

Marc stared. How on earth had the conversation taken this unlikely turn? "I'm not planning on marrying anyone at the moment. There's plenty of time for that later."

"No, Marco," Vito said, "You're wrong. Yesterday there was plenty of time; today the sands are running out. I don't intend to die until I know the Donatello line will continue. In Italy we are an old and honorable family. We trace our ancestors all the way back to the fifteenth century, but now we are the only ones left. I've done my duty: I produced two strong, lusty sons. Your mama, God rest her soul, and I would have welcomed more *bambini*, but the good Lord didn't see fit to send them. Now the only hope for our family line rests with you. I don't say it's fair, but that's the way it is."

Vito shifted restlessly on the bed. "I'm asking you, as your papa and as head of the family, to marry soon and give me at least one grandchild before I die. I can't rest in peace without knowing the family will go on."

For the first time in his life, Marc was speechless. What his father asked was impossible, unthinkable. Vito had been hounding Marc for years to marry and have children. Like most of his countrymen, he had a strong sense of family, and this wasn't the first time he'd pointed out that the Donatello line was in danger of extinction. It worried Vito, and Marc could sympathize, but there were limits to what one man could do for another.

Marco had every intention of marrying eventually. When the time came, he'd select with care the woman who would be the mother of his children. She'd be younger, clinging, maternal, like his own mother, who would be content to stay home and raise their sons and daughters.

Unfortunately this type had never appealed to him as a lover, and he enjoyed his bachelor state too much now to tie himself down to one woman yet.

Not that he was promiscuous; he wasn't. He concentrated on one woman at a time and stayed true to her as long as the relationship lasted. He preferred well-educated, sophisticated business or professional women who were as independent as himself.

"Dad," he began carefully, "you know I'd do anything within reason for you, but what you're asking is not reasonable. I can't just go out and pick up the first virgin *italiana* who answers your requirements for a

Donatello bride and propose marriage for the purpose of producing an heir.''

"Don't be a smartass, Marco," Vito snapped. "I'm serious, and it won't be necessary for you to 'pick up' a bride, as you so crudely put it. I've already found one for you."

"What!" Marco stood up and glared at the complacent man on the bed. *Good Lord, the diagnosis had temporarily unhinged him!*

"Don't look at me like I've suddenly lost my mind," Vito snapped. "Arranged marriages aren't all that uncommon."

"Arranged ma—"

"Don't interrupt," Vito cut in. "Trust me to know what I'm doing. I wouldn't want just any woman for the mother of my grandchildren."

Marco sputtered ineffectually as Vito held up his hand for silence and continued. "I was already trying to figure out a way to get you and Susan together before this came up, but now I can simply tell you my plan."

Marco's beleaguered mind grasped at the flaw in his father's logic—the name. "Susan?" he asked innocently. "It wouldn't work. You don't want an *anglosassone* woman to bear the future generation of Donatellos. You've always insisted Ben and I should marry Italian brides."

"Susan is *italiana*," Vito said. "Her father was my friend, Roberto Alessandro. We grew up together. He married a woman of English ancestry, but their daughter is half-Italian. That will do for me; I'm not a snob."

"That's big of you," Marc muttered in defeat as he sank into the chair beside the bed.

Vito let the remark pass. "Susan is my *figlioccia*, my godchild, but until recently I hadn't seen her since she was five years old. That's when Roberto died, and his widow took the child and went back to be close to her parents in Pennsylvania. Later she married again and never did come back here. Maria and I kept in touch and sent gifts at appropriate times, but it wasn't until Susan graduated from college earlier this month that I saw her again."

Marc watched Vito as he talked, and he could see the way his father's expression softened as he spoke of the child—girl—woman, whatever. "Papa," he said, "How old is Susan?"

"She just turned twenty-two, and she graduated from the University of Pennsylvania with honors. Ah, Marco, she's not only bright, but very beautiful. She's everything any man could want in a wife: sweet and warm, and she likes children."

"Then why don't you marry her yourself?" Marc grumbled.

Vito sat straight up and glared at his son. "You will not speak with disrespect of Susan," he grated, "or by hell I'm not too old or too sick to give you the thrashing you deserve."

He started to throw off the covers and get out of bed, and Marco, thoroughly alarmed, jumped out of the chair and held him down. "Papa, for God's sake, I wasn't speaking disrespectfully. You're obviously fond of the girl, and there's no reason why you shouldn't marry again. I admit she's awfully young, but men often marry much younger women."

Vito relaxed and let Marc settle him again on the bed. "Look," Marc said, "I'm sorry. I didn't mean to either insult or upset you. The nurse warned me not to tire you. I'd better leave—''

"No." Vito clutched his arm. "Don't go yet. Let me finish telling you about Susan Alessandro."

Marco didn't want to hear anything more about his father's favorite godchild. All he really wanted was to find the nearest bar and have a drink—make that two drinks—but he sat down again and tried to relax. "Sure. Go ahead. I'll stay as long as you want."

Vito settled back. "Now, where was I? Oh, yes, Susan's mother died about a year ago. I didn't know about it until after the funeral, or I'd have flown back there. Susan did send me an invitation to her graduation a month ago, and I went."

He frowned and clenched his fists. "It was then I discovered that the man her mother married had collected her insurance after the funeral and taken off, leaving Susan with nothing but the house. Your mother and I had set up a trust fund to cover her college expenses when Roberto died, but by the time she graduated, that was gone."

"Sounds like her stepfather was a first-class heel," Marc observed.

Vito uttered an Italian oath that he saved for special occasions. "She sold the house, but since it wasn't paid for, she barely got enough out of it to live on until now."

Marco was uneasy. He knew his father well enough to know he was leading up to something more imminent than the long-range wedding plans he'd already mentioned. "Dad, are you going to tell me that you're supporting this young woman?"

Vito looked at his son with disgust. "No, I'm not supporting her. Not that I wouldn't have done so, and gladly, but she wouldn't allow it. I finally convinced her to come back to Minneapolis with me and accept a position in the company."

"She's *here*?" It was more of a yelp than a question.

Vito nodded. "She's taken a small apartment and is working as a clerk-typist at the office until something more in line with her training opens up."

"And just what is she trained for?"

Vito grinned. "She majored in business at school. She'll be a fine addition to the company, Marco, and best of all, now that you're no longer needed full-time in Duluth, you'll be working with her. It will give you two an opportunity to get acquainted. Don't take too long, though. I hope to welcome my first grandchild by this time next year."

Marco's mouth opened and closed, then opened again before he finally found his voice. "Oh, *hell*!" he groaned and dropped his head into his hands.

Chapter Two

Susan Alessandro locked the file cabinet and the desk, then dropped the keys into her purse and snapped it shut. It had been a long, difficult day, and she was anxious to get home, take a warm relaxing bath and change into something cool and comfortable.

She picked up her purse and started for the door when it opened and one of the other file clerks came into the office. "Hey, have you heard about the big boss?" she said, her eyes glowing with the excitement of being first with the latest gossip.

"The big boss?" Susan had been with the company less than a month and didn't have the office slang memorized yet.

"You know, Vito Donatello, the owner."

A wave of apprehension swept over Susan. Papa Vito? Good heavens, had something happened to him?

She fought back her alarm and asked calmly, "No, what about him?"

"He's in the hospital," the woman answered. "Been sick and went in for tests, I hear."

Vito sick? He couldn't be. There'd certainly been nothing wrong with him during the week she'd lived at his big, luxurious home until she'd found the apartment. He'd even moved her into it, and just last Saturday he'd come over to see how she'd fixed it up, then took her to lunch.

"Wh—what's wrong with him?" she asked.

The woman shrugged. "No one seems to know. Maybe it's his heart. He puts in a lot of hours and works awful hard. On the other hand, it could be a stroke. Everyone knows he's got an explosive temper." She sounded positively gleeful.

Susan blanched and muttered goodbye as she rushed out of the room.

It seemed to take her forever to get home on the bus, but as soon as she did, she dialed Vito's private number.

The housekeeper, Mrs. Romano, answered, and Susan identified herself. "There's a rumor going around the office that Papa Vito is in the hospital," she said anxiously. "Is it true, Mrs. Romano? What's the matter with him?"

The motherly woman answered in a soothing, heavily accented tone. "There, there, *signorina*, he's just tired and overworked. The *medico* put him in the university hospital for tests, and to rest. He'll be home in another day or two."

The wave of relief that swept over Susan left her light-headed, and she leaned against the wall of her tiny kitchen. When her mother died last year, she'd been left not only an orphan, but without family of any kind. Then less than a month ago Papa Vito had come for her graduation, swept her into his arms with a big bearlike hug and promptly made her a part of his family. She couldn't lose him, too!

The university hospital was within walking distance; she'd shower, have a bite to eat and go over to see him.

Marc parked the Ferrari in the parking lot and strolled toward the hospital. He was tired, but the six-teen-ounce steak he'd just finished had relaxed him and slowed him down a little. He'd been on the run and absorbing shocks all day, and it was beginning to catch up with him.

He'd left Vito when they'd brought his dinner tray and found a small off-campus restaurant that was quiet and served good food. His conscience pricked him as he remembered that he'd intended to call Hilary from the café. Oh, well, he probably couldn't have gotten hold of her, anyway. Real-estate brokers didn't have regular hours, and Hilary was seldom in her office. He'd call when he got to his apartment.

In the hospital he waited with several other people for the elevator, and when it arrived, he walked in and turned to face the door. A blond girl in white slacks and a red-and-white striped sleeveless knit shirt ran across the lobby and slid in just as the heavy doors began to close.

She had a milkglass vase containing several red rose-buds in her hands and stood just in front of and to one side of Marc. The top of her head barely came to his chin, but it was her hair that had attracted his atten-tion. It was the color of sunbeams. Shimmering pale gold, cut with feathery bangs and falling in soft curls to her shoulder blades.

Marc had always been attracted to blondes, probably because he and his family were so dark, but he'd never seen such blatantly sensual hair before. He wondered how old she was. Not more than eighteen, he'd guess, although that close-fitting shirt revealed breasts that were full and mature. He hadn't gotten a good look at her face, but if it matched the rest of her, it must be beautiful.

The elevator stopped on his floor, and to his surprise the girl walked out just ahead of him. He followed her down the hall, enjoying every step she took. She was small but perfectly proportioned, and her graceful walk set in motion a gyrating movement that, combined with the snug fit of her slacks, caused a stirring in a part of his anatomy that was best left unaroused in a public place.

She had him so hypnotized that he didn't notice where she was leading him until she turned into the room he was headed for. Papa's room. He stopped, confused. Who was she, and why was she visiting his father?

Susan followed the signs through the maze of halls until she came to Vito's room. The door was open and she walked in.

He was sitting up in bed, reading a newspaper, but lowered it when he heard her footsteps. A smile split his sturdy handsome face, and he held out his arms. "Susan, *cara*, come give your old *padrino* a hug."

She set the vase of roses on the bedside table and threw herself into his embrace. "Papa Vito, I just learned that you were here."

A disapproving voice from behind made her jump. "Am I intruding? Maybe I should come back later."

She sat up and turned around to see a tall dark man leaning against the doorjamb. His medium brown eyes were cool as his gaze raked over her, and his angular jaw was clenched.

Before she could gather her wits about her, Vito spoke. "Marco," he boomed happily, either not noticing or choosing to ignore the other man's disapproval. "You're just in time to meet Susan Alessandro, my *figlioccia*. Susan, this is my son, Marco. The one who's been working in Duluth since you've been here."

Marco had more or less figured out for himself who she was, but that didn't mean he cared for the way she was throwing herself at his father. The sick, lonely and *rich* older man was a sitting target for that little bundle of temptation. If she cuddled up to him like that very often, it wouldn't take Vito long to start having feelings that were definitely not paternal.

Marc nodded to Susan. He'd been right about her face. It was not only beautiful, but her full lips, slightly flaring nostrils and delicate high cheekbones were every bit as sensual as her hair. "Hello, Susan," he said stiffly. "Dad's been telling me about you."

She looked directly at him, and his breath caught in his throat. Those eyes. He'd never seen eyes that color. They weren't blue, but neither were they green. They were turquoise. Big wide turquoise eyes, framed by long, surprisingly dark lashes, and set below thick brows of the same dark color. They were the most magnificently sexy eyes he'd ever looked into.

Her coloring was English, but her features were sultry, sensuous Italian.

"Come in, come in," Vito said and gestured to one of the several chairs in the double room.

Marc took a seat and spoke to Susan. "You'd better take one of these chairs, too. The nurses don't like visitors to sit on the beds."

Vito raised one eyebrow but made no protest as she slid off the bed and sat down next to Marc.

Susan wondered what she'd done to raise this man's ire. She'd never met him, but Vito spoke so proudly of his elder son that she'd assumed he was a cross between Adonis and the gentle Saint Francis of Assisi. Obviously he was neither.

Not that he wasn't handsome. She glanced covertly at him out of the corners of her eyes. Actually he was more commanding than "pretty" with his strong, squarish face and his slightly overlarge nose. He had deep-set brown eyes with flecks of topaz, and his thick dark brown hair was expertly styled in a modified feather cut that gave it a free, lightly windblown look at the top, then brushed back at the sides to taper and end at his shirt collar. His mouth was one of his most attractive features, and she wasn't sure why. It was neither wide nor short, full nor thin, but something about it held her gaze, and made her wonder what it would feel like on her own, moving, probing, nipping....

She shivered and quickly banished her errant musing.

He didn't seem at all friendly, so she spoke carefully. "I'm pleased to meet you, Mr. Donatello. Your father has spoken of you so often."

He hesitated for a moment, then seemed to relax a little. "My name's Marco," he said. "Mr. Donatello was my grandfather."

Before either of them could say anything more, Ben and Carla arrived, and Carla ran to embrace her father-in-law. Susan was fascinated by the easy, loving intimacy of this family. She didn't remember her own father, and her stepfather had been a cold man who had no patience with children. He'd never hugged or kissed her when she was little, and as she got older, he dropped all pretense of affection and simply ignored her.

That was the reason she'd always felt so close to Papa Vito. Even after his wife died, he'd kept up the letters, telephone calls and gifts that they had always showered on her, and she'd more or less adopted him as her father in absentia.

Even so, she'd been shocked and hurt when her stepfather had shown up at the university that day a few weeks after her mother's funeral. He'd told her that he was taking an early retirement and moving to the West Coast. He hadn't even said goodbye, but just handed her the deed to the house, which he'd registered in her name, and walked away. She hadn't heard from him since.

After the flurry of greetings Ben turned to Susan. "How are things going at work, Sue? Are we keeping you busy?"

She grinned. "You bet. I'm lucky if I have time for lunch."

"Are you getting to know people? Making friends?"

"Yes. The folks I work with are very friendly. I've even had a few dates."

Marco frowned. Dates? Of course she'd have dates. She probably had to beat the men back with a stick. Or did she bother? Just what sort of person was this girl-woman who had captivated both his father and his brother? Had she deliberately set out to infiltrate the Donatello family, or was she really as sweet and innocent as Vito insisted she was?

Ben was speaking again. "That doesn't surprise me a bit. Are these men from the office?"

"A couple of them are," she said, "but mostly I've been seeing my landlady's son, Ryan Caldwell. He's a graduate student in engineering at the university.

Vito had been talking to Carla, but he'd apparently been listening to Ben and Susan also because he broke into the conversation. "What do you know about this Ryan Caldwell? Is he living in the house with you? Are you sure he can be trusted?"

"Dad, for heaven's sake," Ben said, "Susan's an adult. She doesn't need you hovering over her like an overprotective father."

Susan laughed. "It's all right, Ben." Then to Vito she said, "He lives downstairs with his mother, and he probably can't be trusted any further than any other man. But don't forget that his mother lives there, too. She's not about to allow any hanky-panky between her son and her tenant."

"What's this 'hanky-panky'?" Vito asked suspiciously.

"Exactly what you think it is," Ben answered, "and the landlady won't allow it, so leave the poor girl alone to choose her own boyfriends."

Vito grunted and turned his attention back to Carla and Marco.

It occurred to Marc that Susan hadn't said *she* wouldn't allow any hanky-panky, only that the landlady wouldn't. Not that it mattered to him what she did with other men, he told himself sharply.

After half an hour or so, Susan decided to leave and let Vito and his sons have some time alone together before visiting hours were over. She picked up her purse and walked over to the bed. "I have to go now, Papa

Vito. I walked over here, and I want to get back home before it starts getting dark.''

Vito frowned. "You walked over?"

Susan nodded. "Sure. It's only a little more than a mile, and I need the exercise."

Vito looked at his watch. "It's too late for you to walk that far alone," he said in his chairman-of-the-board tone. "Marco will drive you."

"Oh no," she gasped, certain that driving her anywhere was the last thing Marco wanted to do. "I've got plenty of time before dark. I'm a fast walker, and I can even jog if necessary."

"Marco will take you," Vito said, and the subject was closed. "Now, give me a hug and promise you'll come again tomorrow. Marco will pick you up and take you home, won't you Marco." It wasn't a question: it was a statement.

"Papa Vito, that's not necessary," Susan wailed, but Marco's voice from behind her stopped anything else she might have said.

"Come along, Susan. It's useless to argue. Dad's in the habit of getting his own way."

Susan knew he was right and gave in. She leaned down to hug and kiss her bossy godfather, said goodnight to Ben and Carla and let Marco lead her down the hall to the elevator.

They crossed the parking lot in silence, but when they stopped beside the fire-engine red Ferrari, Susan's eyes widened with surprise. "Oh, what a stunning car," she said as Marco unlocked the door on the passenger side.

He seemed pleased. "Like it? I just bought it last weekend. Couldn't resist the color."

"It's absolutely gorgeous," she said and lowered herself into the black leather seat.

Marco shut the door and got in on the driver's side. "It's frustrating not to be able to really open it up." He sounded like a teenager with his first junk heap. "If I drove it as fast as it'll go, I'd probably lose my license. What make of car do you drive?"

Susan laughed. "I gave the Rolls to the butler when I left Philadelphia, and I just haven't gotten around to picking up a new one yet."

Marco had the grace to look sheepish. "Sorry," he said. "I didn't mean—"

"Of course you didn't," she agreed. "It just never occurred to you that not everyone can afford to own a car, let alone a luxury model sport job. Don't worry: I'm not after your new toy, just admiring it."

Marco looked puzzled, as though he couldn't decide whether she was teasing or being sarcastic. "If you don't have transportation, how do you get around?"

"I take the bus to work, like a lot of other people do, and I have well-built feet and legs that are useful for going to the store, and so forth."

"I'd noticed," he said and eyed her slender slacks-covered legs as he started the motor.

She told him her address and gave directions for finding it, then took a deep breath and asked the question she still hadn't gotten an answer to. "Marco, what's wrong with your father? I didn't know he was in the hospital until I heard it at the office this afternoon. Is it serious? When will he be going home?"

Marco hesitated long enough to make her apprehensive. "He's a little run-down, and his red blood cell count is low," he finally answered. "He'll have to learn to slow down. They've given him a blood tranfusion, and if he responds well to it, and the medication, they'll probably release him in a day or two."

Something in Marco's tone disturbed Susan, but before she could comment further, they pulled up in front
of the big old white two-story house with the screened-
in front porch. "This is a private home," he said with
surprise.

"Mmm-hmm," she agreed. "The Caldwells remod-
eled part of the second floor into an apartment several
years ago since they no longer needed so much space.
Then Mr. Caldwell died last year, and their son, Ryan,
moved back home so his mother wouldn't be all alone.
The apartment had been vacant for a while before I
came along."

Marco looked unconvinced. "Did my Dad approve
this place?"

Susan laughed again. "Papa Vito? You've got to be
kidding. He considers it just a step above a tenement.
He wanted me to stay at the family home with him and
Mrs. Romano."

"And why didn't you?"

"Because I'm not family." She was getting a little
tired of trying to figure out if he was insulting her or just
being grumpy. "Look, I'll be eternally grateful to Vito
for his concern and help, but I didn't come here to
sponge off him. I've been taking care of myself for quite
some time now, and I expect to continue to do so."

She opened the door and got out, and Marco followed her. "I like this place," she continued as they
strolled up the walk and climbed the steps to the porch
door. "It's an older district, but the homeowners have
kept it in good condition. The huge old trees and green
rolling lawns give the neighborhood a shady, peaceful
look, and my apartment is small but comfortable. Not
to mention the fact that I'm only a block from the bus

line which stops practically in front of your offices downtown."

Susan reached for the screen door and pulled it slightly open as she turned to Marco. "Thank you for bringing me home. I'm sorry to have put you to so much trouble."

"No trouble," Marc said. "I'll pick you up here tomorrow at six-thirty. We might as well have dinner together before we go to the hospital."

He turned and bounded down the steps and was in the car before she could gather her wits about her to protest.

The following afternoon Susan rushed home from work, showered and changed into a sheer mauve-and-pink-flowered voile dress with a scooped neckline and a wide white crushed-leather belt at the waist. She brushed her long, thick hair and tied it back at the nape with a matching scarf to keep it off her neck. Because her creamy skin tended to be slightly oily, she used only a minimum of makeup: a touch of blusher to accentuate her cheekbones, pink lipstick and a light brushing of mascara on her long lashes. Anything heavier melted in the hot sultry weather.

Minneapolis, the City of Lakes, paid for its beautiful ponds with a high degree of humidity that made the heat of summer and the cold of winter even more uncomfortable than normal.

She was hunting for her white pumps when she heard the front doorbell. She'd told Mrs. Caldwell she was expecting a guest, and a few seconds later there was a knock on her apartment door.

Susan blinked at the man standing in the hall. Last night he'd looked tired, rumpled and more than a little haggard, but he must have had a good night's sleep. This evening he was smooth-shaven and wide-awake. Dressed in a lightweight beige linen jacket and brown pants, with a beige, brown and green open-neck shirt, he looked younger, less intimidating and dangerously appealing.

Her pulse speeded up as she smiled and greeted him, then stepped out into the hall and shut the door. "I'm all ready to go," she said as he stepped back. "We aren't going to have much time to eat and still get to the hospital before visiting hours are over."

Marc answered her smile and made no attempt to hide the admiration in his warm brown eyes. "You're right," he said and took her arm as they started down the staircase. "I've made a reservation at a restaurant just across the river. It's not very elegant, but it's noted for good food and fast service." He opened the front door and escorted her to the car.

The restaurant may not have been elegant by Marco's standards, but she thought it was impressive. The carpeting was thick, the walls were paneled, and the lamps were Tiffany. After the waiter had brought their drinks and taken their orders, Susan settled back and asked, "Have you seen Papa Vito today?"

Marc nodded. "I spent most of the morning and part of the afternoon with him. He's feeling better, and the doctor says he can go home tomorrow if he'll promise to get a lot of rest and not go back to work for a while."

Susan breathed a sigh of relief. "I'm so glad. The speculation going around the office is that he's had a heart attack or a stroke. I was terrified when I first heard about it until I talked to Mrs. Romano."

Marc frowned. "In that case, I'd better issue an interoffice memo on his condition. We don't want unfounded rumors like that getting into general circulation.''

Marc's attention was temporarily diverted from his sensuously angelic companion. Vito would really have a stroke if he knew rumors of that sort were being bandied about. This morning he'd called both his sons to his bedside to demand that under no circumstances was anyone to know the true nature of his illness, not even his housekeeper or his goddaughter. There were to be no exceptions.

Both Marco and Ben understood their father's dictum. He was a proud man and also a powerful one. The fact that he might be seriously ill was unthinkable. He would be a long time acknowledging it. Pity would be totally unacceptable to him, and some of his less scrupulous competitors might try to use his declining health to their advantage.

No, Vito's secret was safe with his sons and his daughter-in-law. The official explanation for his illness would be exhaustion and a mild anemia. The state of Vito's health was a family matter, of no concern to outsiders. Not even an outsider as close to Vito's heart as Susan.

Susan thoroughly enjoyed the meal and the company. Marc not only looked different tonight, but he also acted differently, too. Gone was the suspicion and sarcasm he'd displayed toward her last night. Now his manner was friendly and inquisitive. He questioned her about her background but was equally willing to talk about his own.

No doubt about it, when Marco Donatello turned on the charm, he was almost impossible to resist, and Susan didn't even try. She wanted to be liked and accepted by Papa Vito's family. He'd been an important part of her life even though their rather unique relationship had been a long-distance one.

Ben and Carla had accepted her immediately and made her feel welcome, but last night she'd had the impression that she'd have to prove herself to Marco. Had he changed his mind about her, or was he testing her further? Either way she had nothing to hide, and just being with him made her feel warm and quivery and cared for.

As they left the restaurant, Marco's hand on the small of her back made her aware that the quivery feelings were concentrated in the lower part of her body, and before she could stop herself, she'd leaned against his touch. While they walked toward the car, his fingers moved in a gently caressing manner that increased the tingles a thousandfold.

His touch was so light that Susan wondered if he knew what he was doing to her. Her experience with the opposite sex had been confined to high-school and college-age boys, but Marco was a man—older, experienced and in full control of his emotions. He wouldn't be as easily aroused as the guys she'd been dating. Conversely, his light touch set off more sparks in her than their heavy-handed pawing ever had.

They were late getting to the hospital, and there were only about forty-five minutes left before the end of visiting hours when they walked into Vito's room. Ben and Carla were there, and also an attractive redheaded woman, tall and slender, in an oyster-color designer suit, tailored but feminine.

Although Susan and Marco weren't touching, he was walking close beside her, and she felt him tense when he saw the woman there. Susan hurried over to the bed to give Papa Vito a hug and kiss, so it was a few minutes before he released her and gestured toward the other lady. "Hilary, this is my goddaughter, Susan Alessandro. Susan, Hilary Granville. Hilary is one of Minneapolis's most successful young real-estate brokers."

Susan had stood and turned to face the other woman during the introductions. Hilary was stunning with her red-gold hair, which she wore in a chignon at the nape of her neck, and her expertly accentuated blue eyes.

Susan smiled and nodded. "I'm pleased to meet you, Ms. Granville," she said and knew it was a polite lie. She was well aware of the tension between Hilary and Marc.

There was no smile from Hilary, but her tone was pleasant. "I didn't know Vito had a goddaughter," she said, then looked at Marco. "You neglected to mention her, darling."

Again she turned her attention to Susan, who hadn't missed the significance of the endearment. "Where have they been hiding you all this time?"

Vito answered for her. "Susan's been living in Pennsylvania since she was a child. Now that she's graduated from college, she's come here to work with us in the office."

"I see," Hilary said. "Is she living with you, Vito?"

Susan didn't care for the way that question was phrased, and apparently neither did Vito because his tone was cool when he answered. "She isn't living in my home, no. She has an apartment not far from the campus."

He reached for Susan's hand. "Come, *cara*, sit here by me." He tugged her down to sit on the edge of the bed.

Susan got the impression that he was proclaiming her to be under his protection, and since there were no other chairs available, she didn't object, but she was used to fighting her own battles and would do so if the need arose.

Hilary was obviously no one's fool, and she quickly changed the subject. She walked over to where Marc was standing and put her arm through his. "You're late, love," she said. "Your business must have taken longer than you expected, but we can still make it to the Youngs' in time for dessert. I told them not to wait dinner on us, but we'd be there later."

Susan saw the embarrassed flush that colored Marc's face and knew that the same thing had happened to hers. In fact, she felt flushed all over.

Marc had had to postpone a date with Hilary in order to pick her up and bring her here tonight as his father requested! But why hadn't he told Vito he had other plans? She'd tried to protest, but Vito hadn't listened. That's probably why Marc hadn't argued. He knew his father well enough to know it would be wasted effort. Vito gave orders and didn't accept excuses.

Marc's voice, laced with anger, broke the shocked silence. "I'm sorry you did that, Hilary. I told you I wouldn't be able to go with you this evening, and I meant it. If you want to go to the Youngs' dinner party, you'll have to go alone."

Hilary's eyes narrowed, and her mouth tightened with annoyance.

Darn, Susan thought. Why hadn't she realized that a man like Marc would be involved with a woman? He was in his mid-thirties, for heaven's sake, and he certainly wasn't the celibate type. Now she'd gotten him in trouble with Hilary. Well, she'd provide him with an excuse and a means of salvaging the evening.

She broke in quickly before Hilary could speak. "Hilary, please, this is all my fault. I don't have a car, so Papa Vito asked Marco to pick me up and bring me over to see him tonight. I'm afraid Marc was too polite to tell me he had other plans. Really, there's no problem. I'm perfectly capable of getting home by myself. I can walk; it's not very far."

"No!" Vito, Marc and Ben chorused in unison, then Ben spoke. "Carla and I'll take Susan home. We've been wanting to see her apartment, anyway." He turned to Susan. "Will you mind if we come in and look around?"

She shot him a grateful look, almost too relieved to talk. "Oh, please do. I've been hoarding a bottle of Bailey's Irish Cream. We'll have a party." She sounded breathless but coherent.

"Now wait just a damn minute," Marco growled.

"It's all settled," Susan said before he could continue. "Don't cheat me out of a chance to get some professional decorating advice for free." Her laugh sounded forced, but since Carla was an interior decorator, the statement made sense.

Just then a voice on the PA system announced that visiting hours were over. Marc glared at Susan, then turned and stalked out of the room with Hilary still on his arm. She called goodbye over her shoulder but hung on as he headed for the elevator.

Now what's wrong? Susan wondered. She'd gotten him off the hook, and he could at least look grateful. Was there no pleasing the man?

Susan's apartment was air-conditioned, as was the rest of the big old house, and she, Ben and Carla sat in the living room, which also housed the closetlike kitchen area that was closed off from the rest of the big room by folding doors. It was comfortably cool as compared to the sultry heat outside, and they were enjoying the small glasses of cream-whiskey liqueur that Susan had promised them.

Susan sighed and smiled at her guests. "I can't thank you enough for offering to bring me home. I was never so embarrassed! If only Marc had told me earlier that he had plans for tonight, we could have worked something out. Papa Vito has the silly idea that I'm going to be attacked every time I step outside the door."

"He could be right," Ben said. "You know how dangerous the cities are nowadays, especially when it starts getting dark. Besides, Marc's perfectly capable of standing up to Dad when he wants to. If he'd wanted to go with Hilary tonight, he'd have said so, and Carla and I would have picked you up."

Susan felt a little better, but she was still curious. "Are Marco and Hilary...uh...going together?" That was a stupid way of putting it, and she tried again. "I mean...do they have a relationship?"

Carla laughed. "If you mean are they sleeping together, I would assume so. At least they go off for weekends, and last winter they spent two weeks in Hawaii."

"Oh." It sounded more like a moan than an acknowledgment. "Are they living together?"

This time it was Ben who answered. "No, that's not Marc's style. Someday he'll get married and settle down, but until then he wants to be free of entanglements." He shook his head. "Hilary made a bad mistake tonight. He's not going to take kindly to her assumption that he'd jump to do her bidding."

"But if he loves her..."

"Love doesn't enter into it," Carla said. "I doubt if Marco will ever fall in love: he'd never give a woman that much power over him. Oh, he enjoys being with them right enough, and he's good to them while the relationship lasts, but from what I've been able to observe, he never lets his deeper emotions become involved. It's all superficial fun and games, and when it's over, he moves on with no open wounds or regrets until someone else comes along."

Carla eyed Susan warily. "Take my advice, honey, and don't build any fantasies around Marco Donatello. If you do, he'll break your heart."

Chapter Three

It was several days before Susan saw any of the Donatello family again. Meanwhile she talked on the phone
with Vito for a few minutes every day. He was chafing
under his imposed confinement, which pleased her because it meant he was feeling better.

Susan's friendship with Ryan Caldwell moved along
at a steady pace. He was a nice man, average height,
average weight, with medium-brown hair, hazel eyes,
and a keen intelligence. She liked him and enjoyed his
company. He didn't alert all her senses the way Marco
did, but he was attentive, admiring and a lot of fun.
Neither of them had much money to spend on fancy
restaurants and shows, but they spent hours in the
neighborhood pizza parlor and movie theater.

On this Friday evening Ryan had gone out for a
combination pizza, and they were sitting on the couch
in Susan's living room, watching an old black-and-white
shoot-'em-up Western movie on television while they

ate. Susan had tossed a green salad and provided beer for Ryan and diet cola for herself. They were having an uproarious time laughing in all the wrong places when there was a knock on the door.

Since she wasn't expecting company, she assumed it was her landlady, Ryan's mother, and called, "Come on in." Just then something on the screen sent them both into gales of laughter, and she buried her face in his shoulder as he wrapped his arms around her in a burst of exuberance.

When she finally got her giggles under control, she raised her head and peeked over Ryan's shoulder to meet the disgusted glare in the dark eyes of Marco Donatello.

The shock sent Susan catapulting out of Ryan's arms and on to her feet. "Marc," she gasped. "I didn't know you were coming!"

"Obviously I should have called first," he grated.

She realized how it must have looked to him when he opened the door and found Ryan and her tangled in each other's arms and laughing like a couple of rowdy lovers. "No, no, that's all right. Please come over and sit down."

She could feel the cursed blush all the way to her toes and knew she looked guilty as sin.

As she gestured toward the worn upholstered chair, she noticed that Ryan was standing beside her, and her good manners overrode her confusion. "Marc, I'd like you to meet Ryan Caldwell. Ryan, Marco Donatello. Marc is Vito's son." Ryan had never met Vito, but Susan talked of him often since he was part of the only family she had.

Marc and Ryan nodded to each other but didn't bother to shake hands. Susan could feel the animosity radiating from Marc and said the first thing she could think of. "Won't you join us? I'm afraid the pizza's gotten cold, but it will only take a minute to warm in the microwave."

She reached down and picked up the half-empty platter, but Marc's voice stopped her. "I've had dinner, thank you." His tone echoed his distaste. "I came to talk to you, Susan. It's business, but I can come back when you're—" he glanced at Ryan "—alone."

This time Ryan answered. "That's okay. We've finished eating. I'll run along." He reached over and kissed Susan on the cheek. "See you later, Babe," he said and left.

"Please, sit down," Susan said to Marc as she gathered up food, dirty dishes and empty drink cans from the coffee table. "I'll be with you as soon as I clear away this clutter."

She was painfully aware that the remnants of their meal made her usually immaculate apartment appear littered, and the stale odor of onion, garlic and pastrami permeated the room.

"Would you like a beer?" she asked as she quickly deposited the dishes in the sink, "Or I could make coffee."

"Nothing, thank you," Marc said and seated himself in the chair she'd indicated earlier.

What on earth was he doing here? Susan wondered, as she closed the doors on the cooking area and walked across the room to sit on the couch.

"I'm sorry to have interrupted your evening," he said, not sounding a bit sorry, "but this couldn't be handled over the phone."

"It's all right," she answered. "Ryan and I were just...just..." Oh, darn, now was no time for her mind to go blank.

"Yes, well, this won't take long. Perhaps he can come back later. I understand you've been in close touch with my father all week."

She blinked. "Yes, I suppose I have. I haven't seen him, but we talk on the phone. Is something wrong? Is he all right?" Anxiety quavered in her voice.

"He's well, but unfortunately not as well as he thinks he is. He insists on going back to work, and that's something we cannot allow. The doctor won't authorize it, and Ben and I won't permit it. As you can imagine, Dad is in a towering rage."

"Oh, my," Susan groaned. "I'm sure he is."

She hadn't known Vito well for very long, but long enough to know he'd consider interference from his sons to be rank insubordination. "What are you going to do? Is there any way I can help?"

For the first time since he arrived, Marc seemed to relax enough to sit back comfortably in the chair. "Yes, as a matter of fact there is," he said. "We've finally hit on a compromise we can all accept. The doctor has reluctantly agreed to allow Dad to set up an office and work a few hours a day at home. He'll need a secretary who can come to the house, and he wants you to take the job."

Susan smiled, pleased that Vito would ask for her. "I'd be delighted to work with him," she said.

Marc held up his hand. "Not so fast—there's more. Ben and I would like for you to move into the house and live there until Dad is able to go back to the office full-time."

Her eyes widened with surprise. "Live there? You mean give up my apartment?"

He gestured impatiently. "I'm sure your friend Caldwell can find his way to Dad's house. I'll draw him a map, if it will help," he said sarcastically.

"You needn't be rude," she snapped. "The idea of moving out of my apartment just after I've gotten settled in isn't exactly appealing. How long would I be living at Papa Vito's? If I give up this apartment, I'll just have to find another one in a month or two, and moving is a big hassle. Besides, why do you want me to live there when I'd only be working a few hours a week?"

"Sorry," Marc said, in a more pleasant tone. "My remarks about your personal life were uncalled for. I've been under a strain, and it hasn't improved my already questionable disposition a bit."

He sighed and relaxed again. "Ben and I want you with Dad because he needs someone to look after him, make sure he gets his rest, takes his medication, that sort of thing, but he won't hear of hiring a nurse or attendant. He will agree to a secretary, though, and he'd be delighted to have you move back into the house again. As I understand it, he never wanted you to move out in the first place."

Susan crossed her legs and smoothed her full cotton skirt over them. "As you well know, he's very protective of anyone he considers his responsibility. Although I certainly don't consider myself in that category, he feels otherwise and invited me to live at his home. I felt then that I'd be imposing. I'm not his daughter, merely a goddaughter."

"He doesn't seem to make the same distinction," Marc muttered. "Besides, you'd be paid as a full-time companion, in addition to your wages as a secretary."

She stiffened. "Marc, I wouldn't dream of accepting wages for looking after Papa Vito. I owe him so much more than I could ever repay. He's been guardian angel, friend, and yes, father to me for as long as I can remember. If there's finally a way that I can fill a void in his life the way he's filled the one in mine, I'll be eternally grateful for the opportunity."

Her voice broke, and she swallowed the lump in her throat.

Marc watched Susan as she spoke, which was certainly no hardship. Actually his problem was keeping his gaze off her. She was a joy to look at, and it wasn't only those astonishing turquoise eyes. Her mouth was another distinctive feature. It always looked as though it had just been kissed, or was about to be, and no amount of makeup could simulate that effect. As a matter of fact, if she'd been wearing any lipstick, she'd eaten it off with the pizza, but still her mouth looked ripe and rosy and beckoning.

Damn! He wanted to kiss her so badly that his own mouth twitched. It was a good thing they weren't sitting close together. If he were within reaching distance, he wouldn't be able to restrain himself from taking her in his arms and tasting her.

With a silent curse he tore his glance away. He wasn't the only one who couldn't keep his hands and eyes off her, he reminded himself. Every time he walked in on her unexpectedly, he found her in a different man's arms.

Did she deliberately entice every man she met? Her manner was so sweet and wholesome, but she positively radiated sex appeal. He'd never before known a woman who sent out such contradictory signals, and she seemed to be unaware that she was doing it. Well, he wasn't unaware of it, and he'd better get his mind back to the conversation, or he'd do or say something he'd regret later.

"We can discuss salary another time," he said and hoped that was the last thing she'd been talking about. "I'd better caution you not to let Dad know that you're there to look after him. It will have to be done subtly. I won't attempt to tell you how: you seem to know instinctively how to handle him. He's hardheaded, stubborn, an old-country-type Italian, and if you let him, he'll take charge of your life and run it the way he feels is best for you. Ben and I only survived his loving domination because we are as hardheaded and stubborn as he is, but you..." He shrugged. "You're soft and sweet, and eager to please him. Also, you feel obligated to him. Unless you learn to stand up and fight back, he'll smother you, Susan, and there's not much I can do to protect you."

Susan laughed. "Marc, I'm afraid the 'protection' of one Donatello at a time is all I can handle. Whether you know it or not, you have the same qualities as your father, so please don't add your 'protection' to his, or I'll really go under."

Marc grinned. "You may be right. Okay, you're on your own. How soon can you move in?"

She frowned. "Oh, golly, I'll have to pack up all my stuff again...."

"Look," Marc interrupted. "I have a suggestion. It won't cost you anything to live with Dad, no rent or groceries, so why don't you keep this apartment. Then you'll have a place to come back to once Dad doesn't need you any longer."

Marc couldn't tell her that it was very likely Vito would never be able to return to work full-time and that he would probably need her, or someone like her, for the rest of his life. Marco was sworn to secrecy, but even if he hadn't been, he wouldn't have burdened her with the truth about Vito's illness until it was absolutely necessary. If she really cared as much for him as she appeared to, the knowledge would shatter her. She'd already lost her real father and been abandoned by a stepfather. She didn't need the knowledge that the chances of her godfather living out his normal life span were almost nil.

Susan slapped her forehead with the heel of her hand. "Of course. Why didn't I think of that? I'm not usually so slow-witted. I'll only have to move my clothes and personal things. This way I'll also have a place to come to on my days off." She grinned impishly. "Something tells me I'm going to need a retreat where I can hole up and recharge my sanity if I'm going to be living in the middle of the Donatello family."

Marc's laugh was one of genuine pleasure. "You read us well, *bellezza*. We're self-centered, temperamental, and we yell a lot, but once you've been accepted as a member, you'll be looked after, protected, and in your case, chaperoned, whether you like it or not."

Susan gasped. "You wouldn't dare!"

"Oh, no?" His tone was serious, but his eyes glittered with amusement. "Just wait until young Caldwell comes to the house to call on you. You'll see."

Over the weekend, Susan moved into the impressive old stone Donatello mansion in the prestigious Mt.

Curve area. She was once more installed in the big luxurious room she'd used before. It was decorated in
shades of mauve and cream, with touches of mint green
in the flowered ruffled beadspread and matching dra-
peries. Located on the second floor at the front of the
house, as was the master bedroom, it overlooked the
colorful gardens, stately old shade trees and smooth
green lawns of the parklike grounds. At the back were
more gardens and a screened-in patio.

Susan felt like a princess in the midst of all this ex-
travagance and had to remind herself that she was here
as an employee, not as a guest.

Vito was delighted to have her back, and on Sunday
started setting up an office suite in two of the six sec-
ond-floor bedrooms. Marc, who was helping Susan
move in, objected strenuously. "Dammit, Dad, you're
setting up for full-time work. You know that's not what
Leo agreed to. He said two or three hours a day at the
most, and then only if you feel up to it."

"I've only had the things that I really need brought
over from the main office," Vito protested. "I can't
work without my desk and my files and my phones.
Susan needs a desk, and a word processor, printer,
copier, and the interoffice communications system will
save me having to get up and go get her when I want
her."

Marc was having none of it. "There's plenty of space
for the two of you to work in one room. You don't need
all this stuff."

"Don't be dense," Vito barked. "Susan needs a private place to work when I'm having meetings or con-
ducting interviews."

"Meetings! Interviews!" Marc roared. "That's exactly what I was afraid of. Leo said you could answer

your mail and make a few high-level decisions, not have meetings and do interviews!''

"That idiot *medico* doesn't know anything about the work involved in running a business the size of Donatello Corporation," Vito shouted. "How can I keep up with what's going on at the stores if I don't meet with the managers?"

Marc was beginning to turn purple, and Vito's black eyes blazed with indignation. Susan decided it was time to put a stop to the shouting match, and hoped that in the process, she wouldn't get caught in the middle.

She put her hand on Vito's arm. "Papa Vito, Marc, please. There's no sense in getting yourselves all riled up."

Marc opened his mouth to bellow, and Susan shot him a warning glance and shook her head carefully so Vito wouldn't see. "Marc, why don't you go ahead and bring the rest of the things your father wants from downtown." It was a suggestion rather than a question. "He probably won't need all of it, but everything will be here if he does. He understands that he'll have to take it easy in the beginning. He won't do anything to slow down his recovery, will you Papa Vito?"

Marc and his father both stared at her, then Marc shut his mouth, and Vito relaxed and put his hand over hers on his arm. "Of course not, *cara*," he said virtuously. "I only want everything here so I won't have to waste time running downtown every time I need something."

Marc looked as if he was about to explode again, and Susan glared at him as she slid her arm through Vito's. "Why don't you lie down and take a nap," she said to the older man. "Marco and I will finish setting up things here. I'm an expert on the subject of efficient office arrangement. I took a whole course in it in college.''

"Maybe I will, just a quick one," he said and allowed her to lead him to his room.

He'd been on his feet far too much today, and he looked exhausted, but Susan knew he'd never admit it.

He sat down on the side of his rugged antique four-poster, and she knelt and took off his shoes. He sighed and lay down, and she unfolded the blanket at the bottom of the bed and spread it lightly over him. "Sleep well," she murmured and leaned over to kiss him lightly on the cheek.

"Mille grazie, bambina," he whispered as she got up and turned to leave.

Marco was standing just inside the doorway, and he put his arm around her waist and walked out of the room with her, then shut the door behind them.

"If I agree to take a nap, will you undress me and tuck me into bed?" he asked, and his voice wasn't altogether steady.

He'd never touched Susan before except to help her or lead her, and her whole body reacted to his arm holding her lightly. In spite of his seductive words, he made no attempt to draw her close. If he had, she wouldn't have, couldn't have, resisted.

What was there about this hot-tempered man that attracted her so strongly? He was nice-looking but not classically handsome; he was blatantly chauvinistic, and he was too old for her. He was wealthy, and she always had too much of the month left at the end of her money. Their backgrounds were totally dissimilar. He was strongly Italian Catholic, and, in spite of her half-Italian heritage and the fact that she'd been baptized Catholic, she'd been raised English Episcopalian.

The one thing they had in common was their love for Vito, but even that was on a different plane. Marc was the son and heir, and she was the interloper, the orphan whom Vito felt sorry for.

Marco's hand tightened at the side of her waist to reclaim her attention. "Are you thinking it over, or are you just not going to answer?" he asked.

"What? Oh, I'm sorry, I'm afraid my mind was wandering." She tried not to look embarrassed. "Won't you stay and have dinner with us? It's Mrs. Romano's day off, but I have a sirloin roast in the oven."

She was well aware that she'd evaded his earlier outrageous question.

Apparently so was he, because his eyes twinkled with amusement as he drew his arm away from her. "I can't," he said, "I'd like to, but I have another... engagement."

Ah, yes, Hilary. "You're welcome to bring Hilary Granville, too. There's plenty of food."

He smiled and looked genuinely regretful. "I really am sorry, Susan, but we've already made other plans that can't be broken. Will you give me a rain check?"

Of course they had other plans. The last thing Hilary would want to do was spend the evening with her and Marc's father. If Susan were lucky enough to be going out with Marc Donatello, she wouldn't want to share him with Hilary, that's for sure.

"You don't need a rain check, Marc," she said. "This is your home. You can come and go as you please, but I'm sure Vito would be happy to have you come to dinner anytime."

Marc's smile was gone. "And you?" he asked. "Would you be happy to have me come to dinner anytime, too?"

Her gaze melded into his, and for a moment she lost track of the question as she seemed to be drawn into the magnetism of his tawny eyes. He was still standing close to her, and she felt herself sway toward him just before she came to her senses and jerked back. "I—certainly. Just let Mrs. Romano know when you plan to be here. I imagine she knows what food Hilary prefers."

Susan looked away and changed the subject. "Were you planning to bring the other things from the downtown office this afternoon, or won't you have the time?"

He didn't look especially pleased with her answer as he glanced at his gold watch. "I'd better leave that until tomorrow." His tone was sharp and all business. "Dad's got more than enough to keep him busy here. You will see to it that he doesn't overdo, won't you?"

"That's what I'm here for," she snapped. "Now, if you'll excuse me, I'll finish setting up our home offices. Thanks for all your help."

She turned and walked away and left him standing there looking after her.

Keeping Vito's work schedule light proved to be even more of a challenge than Susan had expected. He was absolutely fanatical about being informed on all phases of the business.

Her biggest problem was keeping him from going to the markets to make sure they were being run properly. Susan was glad she wasn't one of his managers. He must be a real pain to work for, she reflected. In fact she knew he was: she worked with him every day.

The only way it was possible to restrain him was due to the fact that he was totally exhausted by noon, and only put up token resistance to taking a nap. Once she got him to bed, he slept for several hours, and when he finally awoke, she was able to convince him that it was too late to start working again.

On Wednesday of each week, either Marc or Ben took him to the doctor's office for some sort of treatment that was never explained to her, and when he returned home, he went to bed and stayed there the rest of the day. The next morning he was up and all business again.

She got along pretty well as long as she didn't meet him head-on and tell him he wasn't strong enough to work. Instead she gently eased around him, coaxing him to eat properly, get plenty of rest and take his medicine without ever referring to his illness. She babied him outrageously, and although he grumbled, she knew he loved it.

Marc and Ben were in and out, but her conversations with them were limited to business affairs. Carla dropped in once in a while if she was in the area, and she and Susan developed a friendly rapport.

Then, in the middle of her second week at the house, Vito announced that he'd invited Marco, Ben and Carla to dinner on Friday evening. Susan felt a tingle of excitement. Would Marco be her dinner partner? Vito hadn't mentioned Hilary.

She'd better find out for sure before she let her romantic daydreams run away with her imagination. "Will Marc be bringing Hilary Granville?" she asked.

Vito looked surprised. "Why should he? I didn't invite her."

"But I understood they were, uh, dating," she finished lamely.

Vito grunted impatiently. "Marco has dated a lot of women, but I don't have to invite them all here to dinner every time he comes over. Besides, this is a family get-together.''

"Oh." Susan hoped her tone didn't reflect her disappointment. "Then I'll have my dinner in my room. Or maybe I'll call Ryan, and we'll go out for a pizza.''

Vito stared at her. "What the devil are you babbling about?''

"You said the dinner was a family affair." She was puzzled by his abruptness. "I was just thinking out loud that it would be a good time for me to go out with Ryan.''

"Are you being deliberately annoying?" he thundered. "And who in hell is Ryan?''

Now she'd upset him, and she wasn't even sure how she'd done it. Maybe she'd better start over. She didn't want his blood pressure to go up on top of all his other health problems. "Papa Vito," she said carefully, "what is it I'm doing that annoys you?''

"It annoys me that you would deliberately make plans to go out with this—this Ryan when I've just been telling you that I want you here.''

"You said no such thing," she grated impatiently. "You said the dinner was for family only.''

He suddenly looked very tired. "Don't you want to be a part of my family, Susanna?" It was the first time he'd used the Italian pronunciation of her name.

She was beginning to understand. "Oh, Papa Vito," she said, and her voice quavered with emotion. "I want very much to be a part of your family, but I didn't want to seem overeager, pushy. I'm not a blood relative.''

He reached out and drew her into his embrace. "You're the *figlia*, the daughter I never had, *bambina*, and that makes you one of the family.'' His voice was almost as emotional as hers.

He hugged her, and she rubbed her cheek against his soft beard. "Now, mind your papa and help Mrs. Romano plan a nice dinner party."

He released her and walked over to sit down behind his desk. "If you must know, I want you and Marco to get better acquainted. I may consider you a daughter, but I don't want him to think of you as a little sister."

Susan opened her mouth, then closed it as the impact of his words hit her. "Papa Vito," she squealed. "Are you matchmaking?"

"Trying my darndest," he said with a grin. "It's time that son of mine got married, and you need a husband."

"I do not need a husband!" Susan exploded. "I have plenty of men friends, and when and if I ever decide to get married, it will be because I've fallen in love, not just because I 'need a husband' to take care of me."

Vito sat quietly while she ranted, then said, "Do you like Marco?"

"Of course I like Marco," she continued to rant. "What's not to like? He's good-looking, mature and a very nice person."

"Then why don't you want to marry him?"

"Who said I didn't want to marry him, I—" Too late she snapped her mouth shut. Boy, she'd really walked into that one.

"Papa Vito," she blustered. "Shame on you. You're teasing me and making me say things I don't mean...."

"I'm not teasing you, *cara*, and I don't think you're saying things you don't mean. It wouldn't be all that hard to fall in love with Marco, would it? Apparently quite a few women have."

Susan couldn't believe they were having this conversation. "Look, Papa Vito, Marc's a grown man, and he's perfectly capable of choosing his own wife."

Vito grunted. "Marco's an idiot. He's so used to women chasing him that he's spoiled. Just think about it, and we'll discuss it later."

Once he'd planted the seed in Susan's mind, she was hard put *not* to think about it.

On Friday morning the phone on Susan's desk rang. It was Marc. "Susan, do you think it would be all right with Mrs. Romano if I bring Hilary with me tonight?"

Susan swallowed. Of course he'd want to bring Hilary; why had she been foolish enough to think he wouldn't? "There's plenty of food, Marc," she said, "I'm sure Mrs. Romano wouldn't mind."

Mrs. Romano wouldn't, but Vito would.

"Is it all right with you?" he asked.

"I told you before, this is your home. You don't need my permission for anything." She hoped her disappointment couldn't be heard in her voice. "By all means, bring Hilary."

Vito came into the room just as she hung up and looked at her questioningly. "That was Marco," she said. "He asked if it would be all right to bring Hilary tonight."

Vito scowled. "Did you tell him no?"

"Papa Vito, you know I couldn't do that. This is his home."

"It's *my* home, and if I'd wanted her to come for dinner, I'd have invited her. You should have told him no."

Susan shifted uncomfortably. Vito was like a spoiled child when he didn't get his way, and he wasn't above throwing a temper tantrum. "I couldn't do that," she said firmly. "If you don't want him to bring Hilary, then you'll have to call him back and tell him yourself."

"Oh, well," he said petulantly, "I suppose since you've already said she could come, we'll have to leave it at that. Just be sure to wear something really *splendido* tonight."

"*Splendido?*"

"You know, bright, sexy, something that will make Marco forget he's got Hilary with him."

Susan gaped. Was he actually serious? "Papa Vito, you sound like you were putting me up for auction! I know you're kidding, but if anybody hears you talk that way—"

"Kidding? Who's kidding?" he demanded. "You'll never wrest Marco's attention away from Hilary unless you work at it. He can be very dense sometimes."

"I don't believe this!" Susan squealed. "You really meant it when you said you were matchmaking."

"Of course I meant it," Vito said. "You're the perfect wife for Marco. You'd have beautiful *bambini* together. Now be a good girl and wear something pretty. Red's a good color. Or maybe purple. Ah, yes, purple, the color of passion. That should wake him up."

Susan made a choking sound and bolted from the room before she gave in to the temptation to throw something at Marco's scheming father.

Chapter Four

That evening Susan dressed carefully, and she was anything but *splendido*. She chose a dress as different as she could find from the kind Vito had commanded her to wear. It was made of sheer lawn in a delicate shade of blue, and buttoned from the tiny set-in waist to the neck with loops and self-covered buttons. Long full sleeves caught in wide cuffs at the wrists, and the skirt swirled gracefully at midcalf. With it she wore ballet-type slippers in a darker shade of blue that laced around her ankles. She parted her blond hair down the middle of her head, and tied each side back with narrow blue scarves.

Her aim was to look as different from Hilary as possible, and she applied light pink lipcolor and a streak of sky-blue eye shadow on each lid. She'd show Vito that he couldn't stage-manage her life. Marc wouldn't look twice at her in this outfit. He preferred the sexy sophisticated siren, which was, she had no doubt, what Hilary turned into when she got out of her designer dress-for-success suits.

No way was Susan going to try to compete with her for Marc's attention.

She heard the doorbell ring and added a touch of brown mascara to darken her lashes. She hoped that the wide-eyed innocent look would do it. She'd been looking forward to tonight, but now, after learning of Vito's blatant plan to foist her off on to his unmarried son, she wished she'd gone out with Ryan, after all. If Vito said anything to embarrass her, she'd come back upstairs and stay for the rest of the night.

She put away her cosmetics and walked out of the room, but instead of going toward the front staircase, she walked down the hall and took the back stairs to the kitchen where Mrs. Romano and Flora, her married daughter who worked part-time helping her mother, were bustling around getting ready to serve the meal.

Mrs. Romano looked up from her task of arranging fancy delectable hors d'oeuvres on silver trays. "Ah, *signorina*, you look like a *bambina* at her first party. *Bella*."

Susan smiled. "Thank you. Is there something I can do to help?"

"*Grazie*, no. You should be in the living room with the family. Go. Go. Flora will be right in with the hors d'oeuvres."

"Well, I can at least take one of these in for you," Susan said and picked up a heavy silver tray.

She walked through the house to the cavernous cathedral-ceilinged living room where Vito and his family were seated in the furniture grouping nearest the huge windows that overlooked the front gardens.

The men broke off their spirited conversation and stood as she walked in, and all three of them stared. It was Ben who finally spoke. "Susan, you look positively smashing." He took the tray from her and set it on the coffee table. "If you go out looking like that, Dad's going to have to accompany you with a whip to hold back the wolf pack." He hugged her gently and kissed her on the cheek.

Marc was next. His eyes glowed with admiration. "You look about fifteen," he said, then drew her into his arms and whispered against her ear, "but I'm awfully glad you're not. I'd be a fool to let a fifteen-year-old affect me the way you just did."

He hugged her, and she could feel the muscles ripple in his arms and chest and smell the clean fresh scent of him before he relinquished her to Vito, who clasped her with an exuberance that nearly broke her ribs. "*Bella*, Susanna," he said. "You are one smart *signorina*. I was wrong, but what do I know about women's clothes." He winked and hugged her again. "From now on, I'll leave that up to you."

Susan was caught between exhilaration and despair. She enjoyed the admiration. What woman wouldn't? But her scheme to teach Vito a lesson seemed to have backfired.

Marco had not only noticed her, he'd hardly taken his eyes off her, and now Vito thought she'd dressed to attract Marc's attention.

"Is there something going on that we don't know about?" asked Ben, refering to the puzzling conversation between Vito and Susan.

Susan blushed as Vito answered. "No, not really. Susanna was not pleased earlier today when I told her what she should wear tonight, and now I can see why.

This outfit is much more—" he looked at her and grinned "—effective for what I had in mind."

Susan could feel the blush deepening when suddenly Vito changed the subject. "Susan, you've met Signorina Granville, I believe."

He motioned to Hilary sitting in a cream velvet chair, wearing a lime-green chiffon cocktail dress with a plunging back and bodice that did wondrous things to her ample bosom and the smooth, lightly tanned skin of her bare arms and back. She'd brushed her red-gold hair up on top of her head and fashioned it in a loose bun from which long tendrils escaped to cling damply to her flawless complexion. Her crossed legs were long and slender, and she wore white sandals with three-inch heels.

Susan had been right about one thing. She certainly wasn't competing with Hilary. They were dressed as differently as it was possible for two women to dress.

She smiled. "Yes. How are you, Hilary?"

The other woman nodded but didn't smile. "Fine, thank you. I understand you're living here now." There was disapproval in her tone.

Susan ignored it. "Only temporarily," she said, "until Mr. Donatello is well enough to return to work at his office downtown. Meanwhile I'm working here as his secretary."

Vito scowled. "What's this nonsense? Of course you're living here. How can I look after you when you're clear across town?"

Susan stiffened and opened her mouth to tell him she darn well didn't need looking after, when it occurred to her that if she was going to dress like a child, she could expect to be treated like one. She closed her mouth and glanced at Marco just in time to see his grin of amusement. She had a strong urge to stick her tongue out at him.

When dinner was announced, Vito escorted her into the dining room and seated her across the table from him in the hostess chair. She hesitated, surprised and unsure. "What's the matter? Don't you want to act as my hostess?" Vito demanded.

"Well, sure, but..."

"Then smile," he said, "and enjoy."

Mrs. Romano's Italian dishes were superb, the wine flowed freely, and the conversation centered around the grocery business. Susan listened while she ate, but contributed little to the discussion. She preferred to study the people. Off and on, Ben and Carla held hands under the table, a gesture that told more than words of their love for each other. Marc was courteous and considerate of Hilary, but he treated her more like a business associate than a date. The men consulted her about real-estate activity, and she was animated as she gave them the figures and advice they asked for.

Susan also noticed that Vito was showing signs of fatigue. His fragile strength gnawed at her. Surely he should be getting better by now. She'd seen to it that he got his rest, ate properly and took his medication, so why did he still tire so easily? She was definitely going to discuss it with Marc at the next opportunity.

When they finished their homemade *gelato*, a delicious ice-creamlike dessert, Susan stood and suggested they have their coffee in the parlor, a smaller, more intimate version of the living room.

She joined Vito and put her arm through his as they walked. "You look tired, Papa Vito." Her tone was solicitous but not accusing. "I'm sure your guests will excuse you if you want to go to bed after you've had your coffee."

"I'm fine, just fine," he said, gesturing expressively as he dismissed her suggestion.

"Of course you are," she agreed, "but if you're going to inspect the remodeling at the Robbinsdale store in the morning, you want to be well rested."

Susan had learned the fine art of bargaining since taking on the job of caring for Vito Donatello. She knew when to give in, and when to call in debts.

Vito sighed. "You're right: I want to be in top shape for tomorrow. If I don't inspect everything myself, I can't count on its being done right."

Half an hour later he excused himself and went upstairs. After a few minutes Susan followed him to make sure he took his medicine.

As Susan left, Mrs. Romano appeared to tell Carla that her answering service was calling her. Ben's wife had recently invested in her own interior-decorating shop and had quickly learned that a good many of her customers preferred to do business before and after regular office hours.

As Carla left to take the call in the den, Hilary also excused herself and headed for the bathroom. She lingered for a few minutes touching up her hairdo and her lipstick, then walked back on the thickly carpeted hallway to the parlor.

She stopped a few steps short of the open door when she heard Ben's shout of amazement. "You've got to be kidding!"

Marc's quieter voice answered. "I wish to God I were!"

The two brothers were obviously engaged in a private conversation, and as Hilary hesitated, Ben spoke again. "You mean Papa actually suggested that you marry Susan and provide him with a grandchild as soon as possible in case his leukemia can't be brought under control?"

"Suggested, hell." It was Marco again. "He ordered me to. Laid on the full guilt trip; how he had to know that the Donatello line would continue; the fact that he wanted to hold his grandchild in his arms before he died. He has it all worked out. He'll give me three months to court her, marry her and conceive a baby, then the usual nine months gestation period. He made it very plain that he wants that grandchild by this time next year."

Hilary gasped and clapped her hand over her mouth to keep from choking.

While she stood there, Ben gave a short bark of laughter. "Well, what are you going to do?"

She could hear footsteps in the room, as if Marc were pacing. "The only thing I can do. Nothing. I'm not going to be stampeded into getting married just to produce an heir." He swore lustily. "Papa can't understand why I'd object to an arranged marriage. He says it's the perfect solution: I need a wife, Susan needs someone to look after her, and he needs another generation of Donatellos."

There was silence for a few seconds, then Ben spoke again. "Does Susan know?"

Now it was Marc who shouted. "No! That's the one thing Papa and I agree on: she must never know. Even he can see that she'd be deeply offended and hurt. She's too intelligent and independent to ever marry for security and to provide some man with heirs. I'm supposed to convince her that I'm in love with her."

There was no longer any question of Hilary making her presence known, and she stepped closer to the wall to make sure she wouldn't be seen. Whether he knew it or not, she had plans for Marco that were at odds with Vito's ridiculous scheme, and she had to know the whole plot.

"Damn, I'm sorry." It was Ben's voice, and it was filled with pain. "If it hadn't been for that glandular infection when I was a teenager, Carla and I would have given Papa a house full of grandchildren by now."

"Hey, it's not your fault." Marc's tone was compassionate. "These things happen. Besides, the doctors say it's not totally impossible."

Ben's snort was born of frustration. "Maybe not, but I think that after seven years of trying everything modern medicine could come up with we can assume that we'll remain childless. No, Marc, Papa's right. You're going to have to carry on the family line. You do plan to marry eventually, don't you?"

Hilary drew closer to the door. She didn't want to miss any of Marc's reply.

"Of course, but I intend to choose the time and the woman myself."

"What about Hilary?" Ben's question echoed the one in Hilary's mind.

"Hilary and I are getting along fine just the way we are," Marc answered. "I'm not going to be rushed into marriage with anyone until I'm good and ready, and that's not going to be for some time yet."

Hilary heard a door open in back of her and quickly straightened up and walked into the parlor. She didn't want Carla to catch her eavesdropping.

A few minutes later Susan joined the group, and Hilary spent the rest of the evening observing and thinking. Just how innocent was Little Miss Muffet with her lace and bows? Hilary didn't for a minute believe that Susan didn't know about Vito's plans for her and Marco. Look at the way she'd dressed tonight, all frilly and sweet and *young*. Marc couldn't seem to take his eyes off her. Hilary would never have believed him the type to be turned on by the virginal look.

Well, she was sorry Vito was so ill, but she had no intention of sitting by and letting Susan Alessandro seduce her man into marriage. When he got married, it was going to be to her, Hilary. Children had never been a part of her plans for the future, but she'd give Marc one since it was so important to him. But she was thirty-five. She'd have to speed up her plans for convincing Marc that they were right for each other and a long-term commitment was in order.

Vito Donatello had better look elsewhere for a man to take care of his wide-eyed godchild, because it sure as hell wasn't going to be Marco.

The following morning Marco came by and drove his father and Susan to a market in the suburbs where a remodeling project was nearing completion. Marc was wearing jeans and sneakers, which surprised Susan until they arrived at their destination and she found out why.

Vito poked and probed and tested everything within his reach while sending Marc climbing to the rafters, exploring the basement and crawling around the foundation. Susan took shorthand notes as they dictated their findings, and she insisted that they break for lunch at noon. By then Vito's meager supply of strength had run out, but he wasn't about to admit it. Susan had anticipated such a possibility and explained that Mrs. Romano was expecting them at home for the noon meal.

After the men had washed up, Susan took Marc aside while Vito was making a phone call. "Papa Vito can't be allowed to go back to the market to finish his inspection this afternoon. He's much too tired."

Marc smiled and patted her on the shoulder. "I know. Leave it to me; I'll think of something."

Later, after they finished their salmon pasta salad and hot rolls, Marc looked at his watch and frowned. "Sorry, Dad, but we'll have to postpone the rest of our inspection until another time. I hadn't counted on it taking so long, and I have another appointment this afternoon."

Vito scowled, but Susan caught the look of relief that he'd quickly banished. "I'd intended to finish it up today," he complained. "Are you free again tomorrow morning? If not, maybe Ben can come with me. I want to get it out of the way before I leave for Duluth."

Marc stared. "Leave for Duluth? What are you talking about? You're not—"

"Oh yes, I am," Vito interrupted. "I've never missed a grand opening of a Don's Market, and I'm not going to miss this one. You still have an apartment there, don't you? Susanna and I can stay with you."

"No way," Marc bellowed and jumped to his feet. "You're not going to take part in that circus. Leo Tornatori would never allow it."

"Leo doesn't ask me how to diagnose patients, and I don't ask him how to open new markets."

Marc opened his mouth, but Vito hurried on. "Save your breath—my mind's made up. The grand opening starts Friday, and I'm going to cut the ribbon like always. Walter can drive us up in the limousine on

Wednesday, and I'll have a full day to rest before the festivities."

He sighed and wearily got to his feet. "I've been looking forward to opening our first market outside the twin-cities area for years, and I'm damn well going to be there." He turned and started out of the room. "I'm going upstairs to take my nap, but I'll expect either you or Ben to be here by nine o'clock in the morning so we can get an early start on finishing up the inspection."

Marc slapped the table with the flat of his hand as his father disappeared from the room. "Son of a—" he started, then glanced at Susan and stopped. "Sorry," he said sheepishly, "but I never saw such a stubborn, obstinate, inflexible—"

Susan grinned and stood up. "I get the idea, but railing at him isn't going to help. Why don't we go into the den and talk about it. Maybe between the two of us we can at least come up with a plan to slow him down a little."

In the cozy den Susan sat on the wide leather sofa while Marc mixed drinks. He handed her a screwdriver, then brought over his whiskey neat and sat down beside her. "Do you have any objections to spending a few days in Duluth?" he asked. "Dad can't make the trip without you. You're the only one who can keep him on a reasonable schedule. I can't do a thing with him."

The feeling of apprehension that had been with her ever since she'd moved into the house settled like a knot in her stomach. "Of course I'll go with him," she assured Marc, "but I . . ." She looked down and twirled the ice in her glass with the swizzle stick.

"What's the matter, Susan?" Marc put his arm along the back of the sofa and gently caressed the nape of her neck.

The warmth of his touch relaxed her a little, and she looked up at him. He was sitting so close that their thighs touched, warming her there, too. "Marc, what's wrong with Papa Vito?"

Her voice broke, but she plunged on. "You said it was exhaustion, but he's not getting any better. He sleeps at least nine hours every night and naps all afternoon every day. He should be well rested by now."

Her voice broke again, and she swallowed a sob as Marc put his arms around her and cradled her head against his shoulder. "He's a lucky man to have you to worry about him," Marc murmured and rubbed his cheek in her blond hair.

He had an almost overwhelming desire to share his anguish over his father's serious illness with this compassionate and loving woman. He badly needed the comfort she was so willing to give, but he couldn't break the pledge of secrecy he'd made to Vito, and even more important, he couldn't burden her with the truth unless it became obvious. It was too early to tell if the treatment Papa was getting would be effective. It wasn't unusual for leukemia to go into remission, but neither was it a sure thing. He wouldn't put Susan through the torment that he and Ben were experiencing. There was no need to. Not until they knew for sure, one way or the other.

He continued to caress the back of her neck as he spoke. "Dad was not only overly tired, but he was rundown, anemic and had a low-grade infection. He's been pushing himself at a killing pace all his adult life, and you can't undo the damage in a few short weeks."

He loved the feel of her soft, pliant body against his own, and his arms tightened around her. Last night she'd looked like a child, but this was no adolescent he held so close. She was all woman, reminding him in a most elemental way that he was a man.

Susan snuggled into Marc's embrace. Her heart was pounding, and she wasn't sure how she'd come to be in his arms, but she felt right at home there. She'd known that it would be like this, warm and exciting, but she hadn't dared dream that it would ever happen. He hadn't shown much interest in her other than as his father's godchild and companion, but she'd been almost sure that the few times they'd touched he'd felt the electricity, too.

"Have you considered getting another medical opinion?" she asked, and her uncertainty throbbed in her voice. "I know Dr. Tornatori is a friend, but..."

"Dad's been seen by several doctors, honey." Marc brushed his lips across her temple. "They all agree on the diagnosis."

That much was true. Some of the best oncologists and hematologists available had examined Vito, and they all agreed that his illness was a life-threatening one. Marc wouldn't lie to Susan unless he had to. He just hoped her questions wouldn't become too probing.

She put her hand on his chest, just over his heart, and he wondered if she could feel its hammering. She had a subtle fragrance that was light and flowery and clean. Like apple blossoms in spring. He'd never cared for the heavier perfumes so many women wore. They might arouse his lust, but they never set him to thinking of bouquets of sweet peas and freshly laundered sheets and baby powder.

"Then I guess I'm just being silly to worry," Susan said and began slowly tracing designs on his chest with her fingers.

Now he knew why a cat purred when it was petted. "You're not being silly. You're sweet to care enough to worry." He wanted to hold her even closer but was afraid she'd resist, and he couldn't bear to have her pull away.

What on earth was the matter with him? This was the woman he was determined not to marry, and he was clutching her to him like a lover who couldn't stand the thought of saying *arrivederci*. If he wasn't careful, he'd get hoisted on his own petard. There would be no casual loving with Susan. With her it was all or nothing, and he wasn't about to get trapped into a marriage of his father's choosing.

Still, it wouldn't hurt to hold her for just a few more minutes; she needed him to reassure her about Papa. On the other hand, if she kept on stroking his chest, she was going to start up a whole new problem, one he wasn't sure he could control.

"Do you have enough room in your apartment for us?" Susan murmured against Marc's throat.

It took him a moment to answer, and when he did, he sounded as if he'd had trouble understanding the question. "Oh, yes, there are three bedrooms. It's a business apartment, and we leased one large enough to accommodate out-of-town associates. I lived there for several months during the construction of the market, but there were others who came and went. It's empty now, but I'll be going up on Monday. Everything will be ready for your arrival Wednesday."

"Will—will Hilary be there?" Susan hated herself for asking, but she had to know.

He loosened his hold on her and sighed. "I don't live with Hilary, Susan. We see each other fairly regularly, but there's no commitment." He released her completely then and sat up. "I really must get back to the office. Make a list of anything you think you'll need while you and Dad are in Duluth, and I'll see that it's stocked."

Susan felt a deep sense of loss now that she was no longer snuggled into his arms, but she was also elated to know that he wasn't committed to another woman.

Susan and Vito arrived in Duluth at noon the following Wednesday. She'd fixed pillows in the long wide seat of the business-owned limo and insisted that Vito stretch out and be comfortable. He grumbled but did so, and within minutes the gentle sway of the car and the low strains of his favorite symphonic music had lulled him to sleep while she sat up front and talked to Walter, the chauffeur.

Marco was waiting at the apartment to greet them. It was the first time she'd seen him since Saturday, and although he was welcoming and friendly with her, there was no hint of the tender intimacy they'd shared that day.

Susan wasn't surprised, but she was badly disappointed. She'd hoped he might have begun to see her as a desirable woman instead of his father's godchild, but obviously she'd been wrong.

Marc had arranged with the deli department of the new market for a catered lunch, and afterward Vito insisted on visiting the market. The "visit" turned into an inspection tour that lasted all afternoon. On the way back to the apartment they picked up chicken dinners at a fast-food place, and after they'd eaten, Vito went to bed, and Marc said something about last-minute details and went back to the store.

Susan was left alone and lonely, and for want of something to do, she wandered around the large apartment. With a living room, dining room, kitchen, den and three bedrooms, it was bigger than the home her parents had owned in Philadelphia. Her two-room apartment in Minneapolis would fit in the living room of this one. It was tastefully and expensively decorated in neutral tones, but it had the impersonal aura of a hotel. Marc apparently hadn't felt the need to make it his own with photographs and personal touches.

She ended her tour on the balcony off the living room. From the height of six stories on a bluff she could look out over the shoreline and see Lake Superior, a dazzling sight.

She was leaning on the balustrade, watching the lights of the city come on as the twilight deepened, when the telephone rang. Her first impulse was to let it ring since it was probably a call for Marc, but then she realized it could be Ben or even Marc calling her, and she hurried inside to pick it up.

There was no answer to her first low, unintentionally husky "Hello." She tried again, louder this time, and a no-nonsense female voice said, "I may have dialed wrong. Is this..." She gave a number that Susan checked against the one written on the telephone.

"Yes, it is," she said. "If you're calling for Mr. Donatello, he's not here at the moment. May I take a message?"

There was a pause before the other woman answered. "Susan, is that you?"

It was only then that she recognized the voice. "Hilary, I'm sorry, I didn't realize who it was at first."

"What are you doing there?" There was nothing friendly in the other woman's tone.

"Vito and I just got here this noon. We came for the grand opening."

"How long are you staying?"

Susan was getting a little annoyed. She wouldn't have minded answering the questions if they'd been asked nicely instead of being barked at her. "I really don't know, until Vito gets ready to go home, I suppose. Would you like me to have Marc call you when he comes in?"

"Don't bother," Hilary snapped. "I'll try again later." She hung up without saying goodbye.

Marc hadn't returned yet when Susan went to bed at eleven.

The following day Vito insisted on taking part in all the last minute preopening confusion, and by dinnertime his face was ashen. He was too tired to eat, and so he went to bed. Susan had intended to serve dinner on the balcony, but it was still hot and sticky, and the ever-present mosquitos, which some people called the "Minnesota state bird," were out in force. She and Marc took quick showers. Then, dressed—a sleeveless caftan for her, and jeans and a T-shirt for him—they settled in the air-conditioned living room. While watching the news broadcast, they ate the sandwiches and salads they'd brought from the deli.

They were seated on the beige velour sofa, and during the course of the meal, Susan found herself sitting with her back against Marc's chest and his arm around her waist. As she swallowed the last bite of her sandwich, she sighed and leaned her head against his shoulder. "Is the opening of a market always this hectic?" she asked.

He chuckled and nuzzled the side of her exposed neck. "Always. It would be much simpler and a whole lot cheaper to just put up a sign that says Open, unlock the doors and let it go at that."

The touch of his lips sent tiny tremors through her. "Simpler and cheaper, maybe, but it wouldn't be nearly as much fun."

He'd found a sensitive hollow just behind her ear and licked it, making her shiver with pleasure. "You and Dad have fun; I have headaches and blisters. It would be just as effective if we cut out a lot of the frills, but opening a new market to Dad is like a birthday to a small child. He wants to celebrate. That's why I haven't put up too big an argument about him coming up for this one. I knew he'd overdo and probably make himself sick, but Leo agreed with me that it would do more harm to his emotional stability if he had to miss it."

His arms were crossed at her waist, and the fingers of one hand began stroking the side of her abdomen. The muscles deep in her stomach contracted, and in an effort to distract them both without making him stop, she asked the first question that came to mind. "Did Papa Vito start the line of Don's Markets?"

His fingers continued their caress. "No, my grandfather did," he said lazily. "He brought his family to this country from Italy when Dad was fifteen. *Nonno*— that means grandfather in Italian—had been in the grocery business in the old country, but that was wiped out by the war. When he finally settled in Minneapolis five years later, he and a friend had saved enough to buy a small run-down market way out on the outskirts of the city. Ten years later he had enough money to buy out his partner and build another market. He named the corporation Donatello and Son, and took Dad in as a full partner.

"When *Nonno* died last year, he and Dad owned twenty-nine markets. The one we're opening tomorrow is the thirtieth, and Dad has masterminded the grand opening of every one of them."

His exploring fingers had stilled as he became engrossed in his story, but now they started stroking on the other side. She subconsciously arched to accommodate them, and Marc trailed kisses over her jaw line. She turned her head, and his mouth collided with hers in a kiss that started as a surprise and ended as a throbbing need.

"Oh, Susan," Marc groaned and turned her so that she was lying across his lap with her head on his other shoulder.

She put her arms around his neck and lifted her face to meet his seeking lips once more. He cuddled her close and murmured, "Open your mouth for me, *cara*."

She did, and his tongue took immediate possession, both startling and delighting her. She'd never allowed any man this much intimacy before, and she wasn't sure what he wanted her to do.

Her hands clenched in his thick dark hair as he probed the moist darkness until, desperate to please him, she began little sucking movements. He moaned his approval, and one hand cupped her breast. It seemed to fit itself to his palm as if it belonged there, and her stomach muscles tightened into a low pulsating torment that couldn't be placated with kisses.

She squirmed on his lap and felt him shiver as he gathered the silky material of her long skirt and pulled it up until the large callused hand rested on her bare calf. He gently rubbed her smooth creamy skin as he worked his way slowly upward to her knee and fondled it.

Unable to sit still, Susan squirmed again, and Marc caught his breath. "Susan, my God, if you keep that up—"

The strident ring of the doorbell interrupted him, and he snarled an oath as his arms tightened around her.

Susan tensed as the noise continued, on and off, on and off. "Please, Marco, answer it or it'll wake up Vito." She pulled out of his embrace and slid off his lap.

Marc swore again as he jumped up and headed for the door. Susan followed and was standing just behind him as he flung it open.

Hilary, dressed in gray designer slacks and a smoky-blue blouse, smiled at him. "Don't look so surprised, Marc," she said huskily. "I canceled my appointments for tomorrow so that I could accept your invitation to spend the weekend here with you."

She closed the gap between them and put her hands on his shoulders. "Don't I get a hello kiss?" she asked as she raised her face to his.

Chapter Five

Marco put his arms around Hilary's slender waist, and Susan turned hastily away. She was trembling from diverse emotions: remnants of the passion Marc had aroused in her, and shock at the appearance of the sleek, sophisticated woman who apparently had an important place in his life.

"Why didn't you tell me you were coming?" Susan heard Marc say as she walked into the living room.

The door closed and Hilary answered. "I called last night. Didn't Susan tell you?"

Susan continued to walk ahead of them across the living room toward the hall. She stifled a gasp and clenched her jaws shut. She had nothing to apologize for, and she wasn't going to be put on the defensive.

She'd almost reached the doorway to the hall when Marc called to her. "Susan, where are you going?"

She stopped and turned to face them. They were standing in the middle of the room, and Marc was carrying an expensive leather weekender case. Obviously Hilary's. "It's been a long day," Susan said politely without looking directly at either of them. "I'm going to bed."

He had the good grace to look uncomfortable. "It's only nine-thirty. At least stay and have a drink with us."

If she'd had something in her hand, she would have thrown it at him. "No, thank you," she said coolly. "I'm tired, and Papa Vito will be up early in the morning. Good night." She turned and hurried down the hall to her room.

She undressed, put on a robe and went across the hall to the bathroom where she stood under a hot stinging shower. She felt soiled. Apparently Marc preferred Hilary but saw nothing wrong with seducing Susan when Hilary was unavailable.

Not that she was any more admirable. She'd been willing to be seduced, up to a point, even though she knew about Hilary.

She scrubbed herself with soap and a thick washcloth and wished she could also wash away her feelings of guilt and self-disgust. Instead, the very thought of his mouth on hers, his hands caressing her, made her muscles tighten in response.

Angrily she adjusted the shower to massage and let the punishing flow of water beat into her tender skin until the suds were gone. She might not be able to control her feelings, but she could certainly be responsible for the way she behaved. From now on, Marc was Hilary's man, but even if he weren't, he'd be off limits. She wanted nothing to do with a womanizer.

She spent most of the night berating herself for being a fool.

Susan heard Vito moving around in the next room early the following morning and knew it was time to get up. She sighed and burrowed deeper into the comfortable bed. She'd been restless all night and definitely didn't feel up to facing Marc and Hilary.

The thought of them together in Marc's room made her burn, but she wasn't sure whether it was with humiliation or rage. It was possible she would have been the one in his bed this morning if Hilary hadn't arrived when she did.

Susan squirmed and banished the thought. No, such a thing wasn't possible. She wouldn't have let it go that far, even if Marc had wanted it to. She'd never slept with a man, and she wouldn't until she found one she wanted to commit herself to. One who would commit himself to her.

Marc didn't know that, though, and he probably thought she was easy, that all he had to do was put her on hold until the next time. She felt debased and wished she were back in Philadelphia where she'd never have to see any of the Donatellos again.

She forced herself out of bed and dressed in a beige linen dress. They had a hectic schedule this morning: a newspaper interview at nine, the ribbon-cutting ceremony at ten, which would be televised, and a luncheon at one of the big hotels honoring all the contractors who had worked on the construction of the new building. Vito insisted on being a part of everything, and she knew he wasn't up to it. She just hoped he'd give in and come back to the apartment when his strength ran out.

She found him making coffee in the kitchen. He was dressed in gray suit trousers and a white dress shirt, and he smiled and held out his arms when she appeared at the door. "Susanna, I didn't mean to wake you up."

She went to him and kissed him on the cheek. "It was time," she said. "I'm going to fix you a nourishing breakfast before we leave."

"That's not necessary. Coffee's all I want. I'm too excited to eat."

Susan found a skillet, and a microwave-proof rack for bacon. "We'll see," she said as she placed the bacon on the rack and lit the burner under the skillet. "I'll bet when you smell bacon and eggs and toast you'll discover you're hungry after all."

"If he doesn't, I will," said a voice from behind them, and they turned to find Marc, who also wore suit pants and a dress shirt, standing in the doorway. "Good morning," he said, and his gaze sought Susan's.

She turned back to the stove without speaking as Vito returned the greeting and started up a conversation.

Marc talked with his father, but she could feel him watching her as she worked. He hadn't looked as cheerful as she'd expected he would, but then, he was probably used to making love with Hilary by now.

And just where was Hilary? If she expected to wander out at the last minute and find a hot breakfast waiting, she was in for a surprise. Susan would cook for Vito, and for Marc since he was here and waiting, but that's as far as her household duties went. She had been hired as a secretary, not as a domestic.

She put platters of bacon, eggs and toast on the table where the men sat, then poured their coffee and started out of the room. She was stopped by Vito. "You haven't had your breakfast yet."

"I haven't time," she said, not turning around. "I still have to dress."

"We aren't going anywhere until you've eaten," Vito said in a tone that brooked no argument, "so you'd better do it now while everything is still hot."

Susan didn't want to sit at the table with Marc. She couldn't look at him, and she didn't want to talk to him, but she knew Vito meant what he said. With a resigned sigh she walked back to the round table and sat down between the two men.

Marc and Vito continued their conversation while they ate, and Susan nibbled at her food. When the telephone rang, Vito pushed back his chair and said, "I'm expecting a call. I'll get it." He got up and left the room.

Now was Susan's chance to escape, and she jumped up, but Marc was too quick for her. He grabbed her wrist as he also stood. "Wait a minute, Susan, I want to talk to you."

She tried to pull away, but his hand tightened. "Let go of me, Marc," she said angrily. "There's nothing you have to say that I want to hear."

"How do you know?" He sounded grim. "Why didn't you tell me Hilary had called here?"

She pulled again, but it was no use. "I asked if she wanted me to tell you to call her back, and she said no, she'd try again later, so I assumed she'd caught up with you somewhere else. Now let go of me—I have to change."

"In a minute. I didn't invite her here, Susan. At least not recently, and not for the weekend. A couple of months ago we discussed the possibility of her attending the opening day ceremonies, but she felt it would be too difficult to get away from work on a Friday and nothing more was said. I had no idea she was going to show up last night intending to stay."

Again Susan struggled to free her wrist, but he held fast. "I told you, I'm not interested. It's your apartment; you can invite anybody you want. However, you'd better wake Ms. Granville up, or she's not going to have time for breakfast."

Marc blinked with surprise. "Hilary's not here," he said.

"Not here?" Susan stared. "But I thought—"

"I can imagine what you thought," he grated. "If you hadn't run off to bed last night, you'd have known that she didn't stay here. I took her out to dinner since she hadn't eaten, then checked her into a hotel and came home. I didn't sleep with her, if that's what you're so upset about, and I'm pretty damn teed off that you'd think I did."

"*You're* teed off!" she shrieked. "I'm telling you for the last time to let go of me, or I'll—"

"Take your hands off her!" Vito's voice thundered through the room, and they both jumped and turned to face the doorway where he stood, his face livid with anger.

"Dad."

"Papa Vito."

They both spoke at once, but Vito directed his anger at Marc. "She told you to let go of her, so do it, *now.*"

Marc dropped her hand, and the surprise on his face turned to annoyance. "Now look, this is between Susan and me—"

Vito turned his attention to Susan. "Has he done something to you that he shouldn't?" His wording was obscure, but his meaning was clear.

Susan was reeling under the quick transition from embarrassment to anger to amazement. "No, Papa

Vito, it's nothing like that. We were just quarreling.'' She managed a weak smile.

Vito's scowl remained as his gaze skipped from one to the other, then settled on Marc. "What you do with other women is your business, but you'll behave yourself with Susan, or I'll make it my business. Understand?"

Marc's fists clenched at his sides as he glared at his father. "I'm not going to defile your innocent angel," he snapped. "But you're right about one thing. It's none of your business, and I'll thank you to save your advice and your threats for someone who appreciates them."

He stomped out of the kitchen and slammed the door as he left the apartment.

The opening of the first Don's Market in Duluth was indeed a festive occasion. There were carnival rides in the parking lot, a favorite local country-western singer and his band, free food giveaways every hour and a draw in the early evening for the grand prize, a trip for two to Hawaii.

They had complete media coverage, and several city and state dignitaries, including the governor, took part in the ribbon-cutting ceremony. Clowns gave the children free balloons, and the customers could make a meal on the food-tasting samples that were available throughout the building.

Vito took part in all of it, and it wasn't until midafternoon that Susan was able to convince him that he'd have to go back to the apartment for a short nap if he wanted to have enough vitality to survive until it was time for the grand-prize draw. By then her head was spinning and her feet ached, and she wondered if she didn't need the rest as badly as Vito did.

She'd only had glimpses of Marc and Hilary, both together and separately, during the day. Marc had a determined smile pasted on his face, but underneath it he looked harried. Hilary acted like a wife giving help and support to her husband. Everyone but Vito, who muttered something rude in Italian when he saw her, accepted her as part of the proud and happy family.

The August weather was hot and sultry, and back at the apartment Vito slept while Susan took a long, relaxing bath, then dressed in clean, fresh clothing. She'd hoped Vito would accept the fact that he was exhausted and call it a day, but, although he seemed to be in pain and could hardly get up from bed, he insisted on returning.

After a shower and a change of clothes he appeared more energetic, and Walter drove them back to the market. The place was still a madhouse, but Vito walked into the thick of it, and they were quickly separated.

She was scanning the crowd, trying to find him, when Marco walked up to her. He looked tired and a little rumpled, and his lopsided grin made her wonder if she weren't making a mistake by not fighting Hilary for him. After all, they weren't married, engaged or living together. Hilary had no real claim on him, and he sure hadn't been thinking of any other woman last night when he'd held Susan in his arms and kissed her so passionately.

"Don't try to keep up with Papa, honey," he said softly. "There's no holding him back today. He'll keep going until he drops, and there's nothing we can do about it but stand by to catch him."

"I know," she said with a sigh, "but he's already reached the end of his endurance. I can't help but worry."

Marc put his arm around her waist and pulled her against his side. She knew she should pull away, but she needed his strength and the comfort he was offering. "Of course you worry," he said. "So do I. We'll start the draw in about twenty minutes, and after that he's going home if I have to personally carry him to the car and lock him in."

Susan looked up at Marc and smiled, and his breath caught in his throat. She fit under his arm as if she had been fashioned especially for him. It alternately thrilled and scared him.

Last night when Hilary had walked in on them un-invited and unannounced, he'd been shocked at the depth of his rage and disappointment. It was all he could do to be civil to her. Then when Susan looked at him as if he'd committed the ultimate betrayal and walked away, he was hard put not to go after her and plead with her to understand. It was only the knowl-edge that it was his own fault he was in this fix that kept him from berating Hilary and sending her back to Minneapolis. She couldn't be blamed for assuming his much earlier invitation was still open.

Actually, if he were fair, he'd admit that she'd prob-ably done him a favor. He'd never planned to make love to Susan. She was his father's goddaughter, protégée, a member of the family and strictly off limits unless he intended to marry her, and that he would never do.

He couldn't deny that if their relationship had been allowed to develop slowly, over a period of years, he may well have chosen her for his wife. She was almost exactly what he'd always told himself he wanted: young, sweet, maternal, the type who would stay home while the children were small and raise them herself.

The timing was all off, though. He wasn't ready yet to take on the responsibilities of a dependent wife and a house full of *bambini*. He enjoyed his freedom and wasn't going to give it up until it began to pall. If things had gone much further with Susan last night, he could have forfeited his right to that choice.

The roll of drums sent Marc striding off to his duties, and a glance at the temporary stage in front of the market assured Susan that Vito was carrying on with no visible difficulty. He stepped to the microphone and announced the draw for the grand prize.

Susan pushed her way through the crowd toward the stage, but it was slow going. Vito made a short speech thanking everybody for their support, then introduced the country-western singer who drew the winning numbers from the huge container. There were three runners-up who received less expensive trips, then the Hawaiian vacation number was drawn.

It was won by a white-haired couple who had never been to the Islands, and they were photographed and interviewed and applauded. Susan thought that Papa Vito stumbled a little as he handed the happy couple their tickets and talked with them, and she renewed her effort to get to him. When she finally reached his side, he was leaning against the wooden frame that had been built to hold the container for the prize tickets, and he looked ghastly. His face was pasty, and there were deep lines around his mouth caused by his clenched teeth.

He saw Susan and reached for her. She put her arms around him, and he sagged against her. She wasn't prepared for his weight, and it nearly knocked her over before she could brace herself. She called out to a man going by, and he sized up the situation at a glance and leaped up on the stage to help her.

The man wore an employee's badge, and he put his arm around Vito's waist, taking the bulk of the weight off Susan, then called for another employee who was standing nearby. The second man ran over and took her place on Vito's other side, but Vito straightened and muttered brokenly, "I can walk.... Mustn't cause a scene.... Just help me."

He put his arms through the arms of the men at his sides, and walked slowly between them. "The manager's office," he said, biting off the words with an effort.

Susan ran on ahead. Thank God, the manager's office was near the front entrance at the side of the store. She'd been in there off and on during the day. In another stroke of luck, she found the door unlocked and barged in, startling the manager, a tall man whose name she'd forgotten and who was sitting at his desk.

"Find Marco," she ordered in a tight, quavering voice. "His father has collapsed."

As soon as the three men crossed the threshold into the office, Vito's legs gave way, and the other two carried him to the vinyl-covered couch. The panic that had seized Susan left her trembling and slightly nauseated as she knelt beside the sofa and took his hand. It clasped around hers, and he moaned as he attempted to shift to a more comfortable position.

"Papa Vito, what's the matter?" Her voice shook, and she took a breath to steady it. "Where do you hurt?"

She wasn't aware of the commotion going on around them as she brushed a strand of dark hair off his forehead. She didn't know much about illness, but she knew that exhaustion wasn't supposed to be painful. Was Marc keeping something from her? Was his father sicker than she'd been led to believe?

She raised the hand she held and kissed it, then pressed it to her cheek. *Oh, dear God, don't let anything happen to Papa Vito.*

The sound of running feet brought her attention back to her surroundings as Marc burst into the room. She turned and watched him as he stopped and made a visible effort to get himself under control before he continued on.

"Dad," he said and walked over to stand next to where Susan was kneeling, "they tell me you're not feeling well."

Vito started to gesture with his other hand but winced and dropped it to lie across his chest. "Just tired," he said weakly.

Marc frowned. "Are you in pain?" In spite of his effort he couldn't keep the concern out of his tone.

"A little arthritis." Vito's voice was barely above a whisper.

Marc leaned down and put his hand to his father's temple. "I think you're running a temperature," he said, then turned to look at the people gathered in the room. "It's probably just a touch of heat prostration," he announced. "That sun has been pretty hot, but he should rest. I'd appreciate it if you'd all go back to work, and please, don't discuss this with anyone. We don't want to put a damper on the day."

They murmured expressions of concern and started filing out, but Marc called to the manager, "Will you watch for the ambulance? They were instructed not to turn on their siren. Show the attendants in here."

"No hospital," Vito insisted and tried to sit up.

He groaned and fell back as Marc hunkered down
beside Susan. "You don't have a choice, Papa. You're
going to the hospital to be examined. I was afraid this
would happen, and now that it has, I'm the one who's
giving the orders, okay?"

Vito closed his eyes and didn't argue, which fright-
ened Susan more than his collapse had. She glanced at
Marc and saw the raw anguish stamped on his white
face.

It was only a matter of minutes until the ambulance
arrived, and the attendants gently transferred Vito from
the couch to the stretcher. Susan walked along with
them to the vehicle, but when she started to climb inside, Marc's hands on her shoulders held her back.
"No, Susan," he said, "Walter will drive you back to
the apartment."

She looked at him with disbelief. "But I want to go
to the hospital."

"There's no need for that. I'll go with him."

"But he needs me."

Marc shook his head impatiently. "No, he doesn't,"
he said roughly. "Now dammit, stop arguing and get
out of the way. I'll call you as soon as I know anything." He climbed into the ambulance and shut the
door, leaving her standing there watching in dismay as
it drove away.

Susan sat rigid and unblinking in the limo. She wasn't
going to cry, certainly not in front of the chauffeur. It
was her own fault for assuming too much. She should
have known that they were only being kind to her by
giving her a job and a place in their home. They were
strongly family oriented, and Vito took his responsibility as a godfather seriously, but Marc had made it plain
tonight that she mustn't get too close or assume too

much. When the Donatellos closed ranks, she was an outsider, just as she had been in her own family.

Back at the apartment she paced the floor, unable to settle down. Would Marc call, or had he just said he would to shut her up and get her to leave? She felt the bitter taste of humiliation. She really had made a spectacle of herself in front of all those people. How could she have forgotten that she was first of all an employee? Not a daughter, or even a long-time friend, but a secretary who worked in her boss's home.

After three frantic hours the phone finally rang, and Susan pounced on it. "Marc?" she shouted.

There was a pause at the other end, then Hilary's voice spoke. "Susan, this is Hilary. Marc asked me to call and tell you that Vito is all right. He's suffered a relapse of the exhaustion that hospitalized him before, but he'll be released after he's had a good rest."

Susan's lips quivered, and she took a deep breath. "Thank you, Hilary. It was good of you to call. I've been...terribly worried." Her voice broke, and she took another deep breath.

"Of course you have," Hilary murmured. "Try to get some sleep. I doubt that Marc will be home tonight."

Susan's hand was shaking so that it wobbled the phone she was holding. "I will," she said in a near-whisper and cleared her throat. "Thanks again for calling. Goodbye."

She dropped the phone into its cradle and practically fell into a nearby chair when her trembling legs would no longer hold her up. Her head rested against the upholstered back, and she covered her face with her hands. Marc hadn't even bothered to call her—he'd had Hilary do it for him. It was Hilary he'd wanted. Hilary he'd gone to for comfort.

The tears Susan had been holding back streamed
down her cheeks. She hoped that what Hilary had told
her about Vito was true, but how could she know for
sure? The message sounded like the type they would release to the newspapers, chatty but not actually saying
anything. Apparently she wasn't going to get any inside information.

A deep sob shook her. She pushed herself out of the
chair and stumbled down the hall to her bedroom where
she fell into bed and cried herself to sleep.

Susan woke the following morning feeling dreadful.
Her eyes were red and swollen, and her cheeks were raw
from the hot tears that had stained them. Her head
ached, and a glance in the mirror confirmed that her
nose was red and her hair curled in snarled disarray
around her shoulders.

She needed a shower and shampoo, but first she'd
start the coffee. She opened the door and walked down
the hall in her miniskirted red nightgown and bare feet.
There wasn't anybody there to see her, so why bother
with a robe and slippers?

She thought she smelled fresh coffee, and as she
stepped into the kitchen, she was startled to see Marc
sitting at the table, reading the newspaper and sipping
from a mug. She gasped and he looked up, then did a
double take and stood as his eyes roamed over her.
"Susan," he rasped. "I hope I didn't wake you."

She instinctively hunched her shoulders and crossed
her arms over her too-exposed bosom. Thank heaven
the abbreviated outfit had matching panties. "What are
you doing here?" she asked accusingly.

He tore his gaze away from her long bare legs and
lace-trimmed underwear and raised it to her face.

"Where else would I be?" He sounded a little un-strung.

"I thought... Hilary said..." What was she doing standing there in the skimpy nightie that revealed more than it hid! "Excuse me, I have to dress."

His gaze had returned to her breasts and she turned away intent on flight, but he was too quick. "Susan!" he called and bounded across the room to grab her by the upper arms and hold her in front of him. He searched her face and frowned. "You've been crying."

She tried to twist away, but his grip tightened. "What's the matter, sweetheart? You look positively ravaged."

"Thank you very much," she grated. "You don't look so good yourself."

It was true. He looked tired and distraught, as though he hadn't slept much. Well, he probably hadn't if he'd spent part of the night with Hilary. And where did he get off calling her sweetheart?

"You know what I mean," he said impatiently. "You've been crying most of the night, haven't you?"

She lowered her head, unable to meet his eyes. "I was worried about Pa—your father."

"But didn't Hilary call you? I told her—"

"Yes, she called," Susan interrupted, "but I don't believe that the only thing wrong with him is exhaustion. Exhaustion doesn't hurt, and he was suffering."

Marc tried to pull her against him, but she put her hands on his chest and pushed away. "Please let me go," she said, and her tone was cool and impersonal. "I want to shower and dress."

He released her, and she turned and fled.

By the time she'd showered and dressed in white jeans and a long loose-belted blue plaid shirt, she felt more able to cope. She'd had time to think while blow-drying her hair, and she knew what she was going to do.

The tantalizing aroma of ham teased her nostrils as soon as she opened her bedroom door, reminding her that she hadn't eaten since lunch yesterday. In the kitchen Marc was scrambling eggs and toasting English muffins. He turned to her and smiled. "I have to admit I prefer those scraps of chiffon and lace you were wearing, but you look beautiful in that outfit, too. Feeling better?"

She walked over to the counter and poured herself a cup of coffee. "Yes, thank you. What can I do to help?" She wished he didn't feel it necessary to flirt with her. There was no need to put on an act: he'd made it plain last night that she was to remember her place.

He spooned eggs onto warmed plates and added slices of ham. "Everything's ready. Just sit down and enjoy. I hope you like tomato juice—" he gestured toward the filled glasses on the table "—it was all I could find in the cupboard."

She assured him it was delicious, and within minutes he had the food on the table and sat down across from her. For a few moments they ate in silence, then Susan took a sip of coffee and asked, "Have you talked to the hospital yet this morning?"

Marco's brown eyes softened as he looked at her. "Yes, I should have told you immediately. Papa was sleeping peacefully without sedation." He reached across the table and covered her hand with his. It was warm and gentle. "He's going to be all right, honey. Maybe after this experience he'll be more sensible and follow the doctor's orders."

Susan felt a deep sense of relief. Now that she could see Marc, talk to him in person, she knew he was telling her the truth. If Vito were in immediate danger, his son would be too upset to lie successfully. "How long will he have to stay in the hospital?"

Marc grinned. "If I know Papa, they'll have to tie him down to keep him there. As soon as we're finished eating, we'll go to the hospital and talk to the doctor."

We. So Marc was going to allow her to visit his father today. He must be in an expansive mood.

A thought stabbed through her. Maybe the *we* meant Hilary and him. Would she never stop thinking of herself as welcome?

She swallowed the last of her eggs and put down her fork. "Will your father go back to Minneapolis as soon as he's released?"

"Yes. I'll arrange for an ambulance to take him home. I talked to Ben last night, and he and Carla are driving up today." He looked at his watch. "They should be here soon."

Susan pushed back her chair. "That's good. Vito will be pleased to have all his family here." She stood. "Now, if you'll excuse me, I'm going to pack my things. I'm going back to Minneapolis this morning."

Marc looked stunned. "You're what!"

"I'm going home," she repeated. "There's nothing more for me to do here."

He rose from his chair and glared at her. "That's nonsense and you know it. Besides, how do you plan on getting there? I need Walter and the limo here."

In spite of her hurt and growing anger she couldn't help but register this rich man's assumption that the only mode of transportation was by limousine. "I'm taking the bus the way I always do, and it leaves at ten-thirty, so I'll have to hurry." She turned and started to leave.

"Ten-thirty!" he rasped and moved to stand directly in front of her, cutting off her flight. "You mean you don't even intend to go to the hospital to see Papa?"

Damn him! He was actually trying to make her feel guilty. "I won't have time," she snapped and tried to walk around him.

He reached out and grabbed her, and his features were twisted with rage. "You selfish little opportunist." His voice was filled with scorn. "You'd desert a sick man who loves you like a daughter. He needs you, dammit, and you're going to that hospital and pretend that you care what happens to him."

Chapter Six

Something snapped in Susan, and, blind with fury, she swung her arm and her hand connected sharply with his cheek. "You bastard!" she yelled. "What do you know about caring? All you're concerned with is having your orders carried out. You're the one who told me last night that I wasn't needed and to stay out of the way. Well, that's what I'm trying to do. Now let me pass."

She pushed at him and ran, but she wasn't quick enough. He caught up with her just inside her room, and before she could slam the door, he clutched her around the waist and pulled her back against him. "You little hellcat," he muttered, "settle down and listen to me."

She was too furious to hear his words as she fought against his embrace. He was too strong for her, but one well-placed kick in the shins made him lose his balance, and they both fell onto the bed.

Somehow they wound up with her on the bottom, and with him sprawled partially over her, one leg across her thighs and her hands anchored above her head. "Get off me," she ordered, but his grip only tightened.

"We're going to stay here just like this until you quiet down and listen to what I have to say." His words were harsh, but his voice was soft. He lowered his head and nuzzled the hollow of her shoulder under her open-neck shirt.

All the activity had worked off some of her anger, and she knew that he meant what he said. Besides, his lips on her bare shoulder were doing things to her that she didn't dare let continue.

She made an effort to relax, which was a mistake because it also lowered her resistance, and when he brushed his mouth across her throat to settle on the other side, she relaxed even more. "Stop that," she said breathlessly. "You wanted to talk, so talk."

He raised his head and looked down at her, and his face mirrored genuine regret. He released her hands, and she lowered them to her sides, but he didn't move away from her. "Susan, I'm sorry if I said something last night that offended you. I honestly don't remember, but I can't believe I said you were in the way and not wanted."

She tried to argue with him, but he continued on, "I was so upset and worried that I probably did snap at you. My patience and temper are both short, and I was frantic to get Papa to the hospital."

He threaded his fingers through her tousled hair, then kissed her on the throbbing pulse in her temple. "Tell me what I said that hurt you so. I couldn't possibly have meant it the way you took it."

Susan was desperately trying to hang on to the remnants of her rage. Just because Marc had a bad temper didn't mean he could totally disregard her feelings the way he had. Still, he had been upset and worried, and she'd held up the ambulance by arguing with him. "I wanted to go to the hospital with Papa Vito, but you said you were going with him and he didn't need me; that I was to stop arguing and stay out of the way. You ordered me to come back here in the limo and said you'd call me later."

Telling about it brought back the hurt, and she tried to squirm out from under him, but he increased his weight on her and tightened his leg around hers. "Don't fight me, *amore mia*. I didn't mean that the way you took it. You have to understand that Italian men are ashamed to show their vulnerability. Papa wouldn't have wanted you at the hospital last night. No matter how much he may have needed you with him, he would have been deeply shamed to have you witness his weakness."

"Weakness!" Her voice squeaked with indignation. "My God, Marc, the man was sick."

He put a finger to her lips. "I know, but for Vito Donatello illness is a weakness. It may seem silly to you, but it's the way Papa was raised. Don't ever doubt his love for you, Susan, but only his sons are allowed to witness his sufferings, and then only if it can't be avoided."

He buried his face at the side of her neck, and she put her arms around him and held him. She knew it was not only foolish but dangerous to lie on the bed with him this way, but he seemed to be reaching out to her, seeking comfort and forgiveness.

She kneaded the tight muscles in his shoulders. He was heavy lying across her, but she didn't mind the weight. He smelled of soap and shampoo, and his clean-shaven cheeks were soft and smooth.

Cheeks! Oh, my. She'd hit him awfully hard. Her fingers caressed his nape. "I'm sorry I hit you," she murmured. "I've never slapped anybody before. Does it hurt very much?"

He nibbled delicately at her creamy flesh. "Darn right. You pack quite a wallop for such a ladylike little thing."

"You shouldn't have intimated that I didn't care about Papa Vito." She rubbed her chin in his thick dark hair. "Are you like him, Marco? Do you hide your vulnerability from your women?"

"You make it sound like I have a harem," he teased, but the lightness was gone from his tone as he continued. "I'm afraid I'm not as strong as he is. If I were, I wouldn't have been so desperate to keep you here that I'd say hurting things to stop you from leaving. I'd have let you go without ever telling you how badly I need you with me right now."

His words shot darts of pure joy through her. "You need *me*?"

He unbuttoned two buttons on her shirt and pushed it aside to uncover her bare breast. "Why does that surprise you?" His hand cupped her fullness and made it more accessible to his lips. "After Thursday night you must know how you affect me."

Thursday night. The night Hilary had arrived to spend the weekend with Marc and interrupted their lovemaking!

Idiot! She should have remembered. Why did he have the power to scramble her brain and shatter her self-control?

She twisted beneath him and tried to push him away. "Damn you, let me up."

He jerked his head up, but his grip on her tightened. "Now what's wrong?" he demanded.

She continued to struggle. "If you need me so much, why did you spend last night with Hilary?"

The surprise on his face had to be genuine. "What in hell are you talking about? I was at the hospital until one o'clock, and then I came back here and went to bed." He swore. "I shouldn't have resisted the temptation to crawl into your bed instead of my own. Then you'd have known for damn sure where I was spending the night, and we wouldn't have been sleeping."

She lay still. "But Hilary said . . ." She stopped, too confused and relieved to go on.

Marc sighed, and she felt his body begin to relax again. "All right, honey, tell me what Hilary said."

"Well she—she said I should get some sleep, that you probably wouldn't be coming home all night."

"And you assumed that meant I was staying with her at the hotel." It was a statement, not a question.

"Well, why shouldn't I?" Her tone was defensive. "You didn't even bother to call me yourself, although you must have known I'd want to talk to you, not her."

"Ah, Susan." He sounded exasperated. "When are you going to stop making snap judgments and start giving me the benefit of the doubt? I phoned Hilary because she was catching an early flight to Minneapolis this morning, and I'd promised to take her to the airport. With Dad's condition so uncertain, I had to let her know that I couldn't be counted on to be free when she had to leave. I was using the public phone in the emergency area while Papa was being transferred to his room, and there were people waiting, so I asked her to give you the message.

"It seemed selfish to monopolize the phone when others were also trying to contact anxious relatives. She was only telling you what I told her, that I didn't know how long it would be before I'd feel reassured enough to leave the hospital."

Susan felt awful. She really had misjudged him. She was thinking of herself when he was all torn up over his father's collapse. How could she have been so selfish and short-sighted?

She put her hand on the back of his head and drew it down on her shoulder, then cradled it there. "I'm sorry, darling," she murmured, "and also ashamed. I should have understood that your concern for your father was all you could handle just then. I didn't hear you come in. I must have been asleep."

He'd taken possession of her breast again and stroked it softly. "You were. I looked in on you to make sure you were all right." His tongue caressed her nipple, and she felt it harden. "You were all curled up in a ball with one hand under your cheek. I wasn't kidding when I said I had trouble resisting the temptation to crawl in with you. It wasn't lust I was feeling; I was too exhausted for that. I just needed to curl up around you and hold you while we both slept."

He took the tip of her breast in his mouth and sucked gently, sending ripples of pleasure all the way to her toes. Her arms tightened around him, and she stiffened. "Marc." It was a combination gasp and endearment. "You—you mustn't do that. I—I can't ..."

Reluctantly he lifted his head and drew the shirt back over her. "I know," he said huskily as he refastened the buttons. "Don't be afraid. I promise to behave." His eyes were dark with desire.

She cupped his face with her hands and kissed him on the cleft in his chin. "I'm not afraid of you." She looked away shyly. "I'm afraid of myself. I know you wouldn't go any further than I'd let you, but I'm not sure I'd remember to say stop. You—" she paused and ran her tongue over her lower lip "—you make me feel things I've never felt before, and I—I'm apt to forget."

Marc looked down at Susan's flushed young face and was swept by a mixture of shame and frustration. Her chastity was precious, to be protected at all costs, but he wanted her with a fierceness that was frightening.

At times like this he felt like a dirty old man, but it was next to impossible to keep his hands off her. Especially when she provoked him. She did that frequently with a glance, or a smile, or a touch. She had an innocent rhythm to her movements that was calculated to drive a man up the wall. He knew she didn't do any of it intentionally and that she was unaware of the magnetism of her sensuality, but that didn't make it any easier to quiet his rampant male response.

She was a beautiful young woman ripe for the taking, but she wanted marriage, babies and a lifetime of fidelity. All he wanted was to douse the fire in his loins.

He wasn't going to seduce her, but neither could he stay away from her. He had to touch her now and then, hold her, kiss her. He knew it was selfish. She was attracted to him; she'd just told him as much. He should give her his *"We'll always be good friends, but I'm not the man for you"* speech and get out of her life. If he were smart, he'd go to Hilary and apologize for neglecting her. They'd had a great relationship. She didn't expect anything of him but a good time. Unfortunately his passion for her had disappeared since Papa had thrust Susan at him, and now he was placed in the impossible position of burning for the woman he couldn't have, and not responding to the woman he could.

Susan stirred in his arms, and he bent his head and kissed her lips. They were warm and moist, and he wanted to lose himself in her mouth and her arms and the mystery of her chaste body. He wanted it so badly that he had to force himself to keep his hands on neutral territory and break off the kiss.

"You're so sweet and loving," he murmured. "It's no wonder Dad brought you back here where he can look after you. Unfortunately he hadn't counted on having to protect you from me."

That wasn't what Susan wanted to hear. "I'm not a child who has to be looked after," she muttered, "and neither am I in the habit of making out on the bed with every man I meet." She tried to push him away again, but he wouldn't budge. "Especially not with another woman's man."

"What's that supposed to mean?" he grumbled and rolled the bulk of his weight off her, but he kept her pinned down with his leg and his arm.

"It means exactly what I said. You're Hilary's man, and it's not very honorable of you to keep coming on to me." This time she managed to release herself and sit up.

"I'm not *Hilary's man*," he objected, "and now who's being chauvinistic? I'm getting tired of telling you that Hilary and I aren't committed to each other."

"Then don't tell me," she snapped. "It doesn't make any sense, anyway. You two have a long-term relationship, and in my book that's a commitment. I don't have to sneak around behind another woman's back to get a man, so please, just leave me alone."

She bounded off the bed, afraid Marc might grab her, but he didn't. Instead he got up, too, and tucked in the shirt that had pulled loose from his trousers.

She was right, dammit. Even though he wasn't living with Hilary, he'd given her reason to believe he wouldn't play around with other women.

He winced. "Play around" had a nasty sound, and that wasn't what he was doing with Susan, but it probably seemed that way to her. Hell, how could he expect her to understand his feelings when he didn't understand them himself? One thing was certain. He was either going to have to stay away from her or break up with Hilary, and both options had undesirable consequences that he didn't want to think about.

Ben and Carla arrived a few minutes later, and the four of them went to the hospital to visit Vito. The head of his bed was partially raised, but he looked pale and ill.

Susan's footsteps dragged as she entered his room, and she hung back as his sons and daughter-in-law hurried to greet him in the usual emotional Donatello manner. When they were finished, Vito looked around. "Where's...?" His wandering gaze settled on Susan by the door. "Susanna," he said and held out his hand, "aren't you going to give your old *padrino* a hug?"

His voice was subdued, as though it were an effort to speak. Susan raced across the room and practically threw herself into his outstretched arms. He clasped her to him, and she buried her face in his shoulder. "Oh, Papa Vito, I've been so worried."

Vito patted her comfortingly. "Ah, *mia figlia*, there's nothing to worry about, just a little too much excitement and a touch of arthritis. I'll be out of here in a day or two, and then we can go back home."

Susan resolved to control her fear. She raised her head and kissed his bearded cheek. "Cross you heart?" she asked with a wavering smile.

"Scouts' honor," he answered and held up his fingers in the Boy Scout sign.

Their shared chuckle broke the somber tension, and she slid off the bed and walked over to the window while Ben questioned his father about the grand opening of the new market. Marc slipped quietly out of the room and was gone for about fifteen minutes. He returned as quietly as he'd left and walked over to stand beside Susan. "I just talked to the doctor," he told her. "He says Papa can be transferred to Mercy hospital in Minneapolis tomorrow, and then it will be up to Dr. Tornatori when he can be released."

She saw the anxiety in Marc's expressive eyes. Her fingers itched to reach out and touch him, and she curled them into her palms. "Will he be all right?"

He looked down at her, and she was sure his smile was meant to be reassuring, but it didn't quite come off. "He will be if he stays in bed for a few more days, and then takes it very easy until he gets his strength back. We're going to have to make him slow down, and I haven't the vaguest idea of how to go about it."

Susan frowned. "Maybe you should dismantle the office at home and send me back to the filing department downtown. There's not much he can do if all his records and equipment are taken away."

Marc shook his head. "You haven't seen Vito in one of his rages. He'd blow a blood vessel for sure, but not

before he'd fired me and written me out of his will."
Marc grinned at her skeptical expression. "I'm not exaggerating—ask Ben. We can't oppose him head-on that way: it could do a great deal of physical as well as emotional harm. I'm sorry, but I'm afraid it's going to be up to you to see that he doesn't overdo."

Her eyes widened. "Me! You can see how inept I am at controlling him. He wound up in the hospital again."

The magnetic pull between them was almost irresistible. They were standing close but not touching, and the tension was agonizing. She'd told him to leave her alone, but now all she could think of was the feel of his arms around her, of his body covering hers, his hands caressing her breast.

He felt it, too. She could see it in the strained expression on his face and the hunger that looked out of his eyes.

Darn it, why was he putting them both through this? If he wanted her, then why didn't he break it off with Hilary? He'd insisted there was no commitment between them, but he acted as if there were.

"You've done an incredible job of taking care of him," Marc said, breaking into her musing. "It's my fault he's had a relapse. I let my compassion overcome my common sense when I allowed him to come up here for the opening. I knew how badly he wanted to, but for the sake of his health I should have insisted he stay home."

He jammed his fists into his pockets and turned away from her to look out the window.

She wanted to put her arms around his waist and lean her head against his broad back. Instead she turned and looked out the window, too. "You're not to blame, Marc." She could hear the unusual throaty timbre of her voice. "I'm not sure you could have stopped him if you'd tried." She switched to a lighter tone. "You may not have noticed, but your father does pretty much as he darn well pleases."

He glanced at her, and the corners of his mouth twitched with amusement. "That fact has been brought to my attention a time or two," he said dryly. "Unfortunately, I haven't yet learned to outshout him."

"Oh, you're coming along beautifully," she teased. "Take it from one who's heard you try. With a little more practice the two of you will break eardrums all up and down the block when you start yelling at each other."

A grin split Marc's face. "Is that so," he said and reached over to tickle her with both hands.

She yelped with laughter and grabbed his arms. "Yes, that's so," she said as his marauding fingers roamed over her sensitive body, sending her into gales of laughter.

When Ben and Carla prepared to drive back to Minneapolis that evening, Susan packed to leave with them.

Marc objected. "I'll be following the ambulance tomorrow, and you can ride back with me."

Susan shook her head. "Be reasonable, Marc. You know what would happen if I spent the night here in the apartment alone with you. I've told you how I feel, and I'm not going to argue about it."

He put his hand under her chin and tipped her head so that she looked up at him. "I'm not going to force myself on you, honey."

She moistened her lips with the tip of her tongue. "You wouldn't have to. You're an extremely talented lover, and I'm not sophisticated enough to play in your league."

Her eyes closed to shut out his probing gaze. She felt shy about saying these things to him. She was revealing far more than she wanted to, but it was the only way she could make him understand.

There were times when being a twenty-two-year-old virgin was a pain in the...whatever. Most of the men she'd dated thought she was frigid, and she'd even begun to wonder about that herself. Then Marc came along and banished all doubts about her ability to feel passion. She didn't know if it was love, but he had only to look at her with those soft brown eyes to make her throb. When he touched her, she melted, and when he kissed her, she was lost.

As though reading her mind, he lowered his head and brushed her trembling lips with his own. "Your innocence is precious to me, *mia puppida*, but you're right; it's best that you go with Ben and Carla." He kissed her again, this time lingeringly. When he said goodbye, she had to force herself to leave him.

Later, as they rode through the twilight, she asked Carla what *mia puppida* meant. "It means 'my little doll,'" Carla said and grinned knowingly.

The following morning, Sunday, Susan woke to a clear sunny day in the bedroom of her own apartment. She'd asked Ben to bring her there when they'd gotten in last night, and he'd done so without asking any questions.

She got out of bed and went to the window overlooking the neatly landscaped backyards of the neighbors. She liked the freedom that living in her own apartment gave her.

Not that she wasn't permitted to do as she pleased at the Donatello mansion, but the size of it and the formal luxury intimidated her. She'd never felt free to sleep late or go barefoot or rummage in the refrigerator for a snack between meals. Although Vito went out of his way to make her feel at home, she was living in the house as an employee.

It was midafternoon before Marco called. By then Susan had given the apartment a thorough cleaning and had lunched downstairs with her landlady, Mrs. Caldwell, and Ryan. They'd brought her up to date on all the neighborhood gossip and Ryan's summer-school classes, but although she'd left her door open so she could hear her telephone, she'd been uneasy. She'd excused herself as soon as she and Ryan had washed the dishes and spent the rest of the time sitting by the phone, reading and waiting for it to ring.

When it did, Marc sounded disgruntled. "What are you doing over there? When I got here, Mrs. Romano said you didn't come home last night."

Susan sighed. "Good afternoon, Marc, it's nice to hear your voice, too," she said sarcastically. "Now, what on earth are you talking about?"

"I'm talking about the fact that I'm at the house and you're not. Mrs. Romano says she hasn't seen you since Ben brought you back. You didn't say anything about going to your apartment when you left Duluth yesterday."

He sounded like a father talking to his fourteen-year-old child.

"There was no reason for me to go back to the house," she said patiently. "Papa Vito isn't even there, and today's Sunday, my day off, remember? Besides, I called Mrs. Romano this morning to tell her I was back, and where you could get in touch with me. I've been waiting for your call. Is Papa Vito all right? Was the trip very hard on him?"

Marc muttered something in Italian that she assumed wasn't usually said in polite conversation, then told her what she wanted to know. "Yes, the trip was tiring for him, but he was sleeping when I left the hospital. Leo will be in later to examine him. I'll be right over to get you."

He hung up without giving her a chance to answer.

Susan took a quick shower and had just finished dressing in a pink-and-gray short one-piece romper when Marc arrived. His gaze traveled over her long slender bare legs, then rested on the snug-fitting bodice before it reached her face.

"Susan, why do you insist on being so contrary?" he grumbled as he walked past her into the apartment. "When I got back, I naturally assumed you'd be at the house. I don't enjoy having to chase all over the city to find you."

"I didn't expect you to, Marc," she said, trying to keep the annoyance out of her tone. "Ben knew where I was, and so did Mrs. Romano. You told me what I wanted to know on the phone; there was no need for you to come over." She opened the sliding door across the tiny kitchenette. "I have Irish cream whiskey and cola; which do you want?"

In spite of his irritation with her, Marc smiled. He'd thought there were no women like Susan left in the world. She didn't drink except once in a while socially, she didn't smoke, she seldom swore, and she didn't sleep around.

Maybe Papa was right. Maybe he should marry her before she got away, and start that family he intended to have eventually. He wasn't likely to find another woman who so nearly fit his image of the perfect wife. At least not one who fired him up the way she did. He'd been silently berating her all the way over here, but the minute she opened the door he was so glad to see her again that all he'd wanted was to take her in his arms and hold her.

"I'll have the cola with ice," he said in answer to her question, then lowered himself onto the only comfortable upholstered chair in the room. If he sat on the couch and she sat down beside him, he'd never be able to keep his hands off her.

Marc hadn't seen her in shorts before, and the sight of her shapely thighs was making him extremely uncomfortable. His palms itched to caress them; they looked so smooth and creamy and softly rounded. It didn't help to look elsewhere, because higher up the swell of her ample breasts under the clinging material set his teeth on edge. Damn! He hadn't been this unstrung by the sight of a woman's legs for fifteen years.

Susan handed Marc his glass of cola and settled down on the couch with her own. What was the matter with him? she wondered. Why did it matter to him that she'd come here last night instead of the house? He was worried and upset about his father—that she could understand—but why was he taking it out on her?

Well, there was only one way to find out. She took a sip of her cool drink and asked, "What's wrong, Marc? Why are you so grumpy? Is there something you're not telling me about Papa Vito's condition?"

Marco leaned back in the chair and closed his eyes. "I'm sorry, I didn't mean to snap at you. I guess I'm just tired. Papa's fine, but the strain of trying to oversee the construction in Duluth, keep up with the business here and cope with his illness seems to be getting to me.''

Her concerned gaze roamed over him. He looked exhausted. Why hadn't she noticed it before? There were bluish circles under his eyes and lines of weariness around his mouth. It occurred to her that his temperament was a lot like his father's. He no doubt drove himself past his limit. What he needed was a wife who would slow him down and see that he kept regular hours. A woman to love him and take care of him. A woman like her.

She snapped her attention away from that dangerous subject. ''Why don't you go home and go to bed?'' Much to her consternation, her voice throbbed with concern, and she cleared her throat. ''I'm going to the hospital this evening, and I'll explain to Papa Vito.''

Marc opened his eyes and looked at her. God, what he wouldn't give to stretch out on his bed with her in his arms. He wouldn't even need to make love to her. Just cuddling her against him and knowing she would still be there when he woke up would be heaven.

Enough! In another few minutes he was going to say or do something that would make her think worse of him than she already did.

He finished his drink and set the glass on the floor. ''When you're ready, we'll go back to the house, and I'll take a nap there until dinnertime. Then we'll go to the hospital together.''

Susan was sorely tempted. Not only to go home with him, but more immediately to go over and sit on the arm of his chair, cradle his head between her breasts and soothe away his tension. He'd like that, she was almost sure, but she doubted that it would end there. Besides, she'd told him to leave her alone, and she had nothing but contempt for a woman who teased, a person who pulled away but sent out inviting signals. She wouldn't do that to Marc; she cared too much for him.

She looked down and swirled the ice around in her glass. "I'm not going back to the house tonight, Marc. I'm going to stay here while Papa Vito's in the hospital."

He looked at her as though she'd taken leave of her senses. "That's out of the question," he grated. "You still have an office to run at the house, whether Dad's there or not."

"I realize that, and I'll be there from nine until five, but then I'm coming back here. There's no need for me to stay at the house until your father goes home, and I feel more comfortable here in my own apartment."

Marc's shoulders slumped as he sat forward and rested his elbows on his thighs. "Don't you like us, Susan?" His voice was low. "You've made it plain that you haven't much use for me, but surely Papa and Ben haven't offended you. Why are you punishing them?"

Susan was stunned. Where did he ever get such a wrong idea? "Marc, you can't possibly believe that!" she sputtered indignantly. "Why, Papa Vito's the father I never had. I love the whole crazy Donatello family, including you. Ben and Carla are like brother and sister to me."

"And me?" Marc asked. "Where do I fit in? What am I to you?"

Susan was silent for a moment. "Try as I may, I can't fit you into any category. Certainly not brother. I'm not even sure that you want to be my friend. Maybe that's why I feel out of place in your father's home. I need to live my own life. I can't exist in the shadow of the Donatellos, never knowing from one day to the next whether

I'm considered family, friend or just another employee.''

He sighed. "If you weren't so sensitive, you'd understand that the reason I'm sometimes abrupt with you is because I do consider you as family. Papa, Ben, Carla and I yell at each other all the time. None of us takes offense because we understand that it's just a way of letting off steam. We're an emotional group, and we don't try to hide our feelings among ourselves. It's outsiders who see only the polite side of us. We don't care enough about them to get upset."

He spoke softly, with an underlying despondency, and his words sent a quiver reverberating through her responsive psyche. He was as confused as she about their relationship! The idea that he might be unsure of himself had never occurred to her.

Without stopping to weigh the consequences, she got up and went to him. She knelt between his knees and took his hands in hers as she looked into his eyes. "Marc," she said gently, "it's because you're special to me that I'm so sensitive to your moods. We never raised our voices in my family. When Mom and my stepfather were angry at each other, they didn't speak at all. I grew up thinking all families were like that." Her smile was shaky. "You'll have to give me time to adjust to your combustible emotions. Part of the time you're mad at me, and at other times you're indifferent."

With a low groan Marc pulled her up onto his lap and cradled her against him in an embrace that nearly squeezed the breath out of her. Any thought of resistance died aborning as her body quickened. She put her arms around his neck and savored the firm texture of his dark brown hair under her hands. "I'm never indifferent to you, *cara*," he murmured as he nuzzled her ear.

"You should know that: you spend most of your time fending off my advances. You have me in such a state that I've either got to yell at you or make love to you."

Chapter Seven

Marc took Susan's advice and went back to his own apartment, showered and went to bed, even though it was only eight o'clock. He hoped to get at least ten hours of uninterrupted sleep. He doubted if he'd had that much all put together in the past three nights. Between Hilary's unexpected appearance, Papa's collapse and Susan's refusal to stay on with him in Duluth, his nerves were about shot.

Now, even after the shower, he was too aroused to sleep. Earlier, when Susan had knelt in front of him and told him he was special to her, his carefully structured control had snapped. Once he had her on his lap, with her softly rounded body so intimately pressed against him, he forgot everything but the feel and the taste and the fragrance of her. By the time he realized that his blood was pounding and his fingers were probing under the leg of her shorts, it was almost too late. Only by practically dumping her on the floor and getting out of there as quickly as possible had he managed to restrain himself.

He shivered and rolled over to sit on the edge of the bed. The woman was driving him crazy, and the only solution was unacceptable. If he gave in to her sensual seduction and Papa's demands and married her, he'd very likely come to resent both of them. He wasn't ready for marriage and the restrictions and responsibilities it entailed.

He got up and started wandering around the room. Granted, it was time for him to settle down, start the family he wanted. Every time he thought of Vito and his frantic request for a grandchild before he died to assure the continuation of the Donatello line, he felt selfish and guilty, but marriage vows were sacred. He'd drifted away from attending mass regularly in the past few years, but he'd been taught well. Marriage was for life and not to be entered into lightly.

He stopped in front of the massive cherry-wood dresser and picked up a framed photograph that was always kept there, then turned on the light so he could see the features of the man and woman in detail. Papa and Mama on their twenty-fifth wedding anniversary. She'd been forty-two, and Papa forty-seven, but they had that special glow reserved for newlyweds.

Maria Donatello had been a seventeen-year-old bride, shy and innocent. After twenty-five years she had matured into a beautiful woman, confident and secure, with a husband and two grown sons who adored her. Vito had married her because it was what their families wished, but they'd learned to love each other with a deep and abiding love that was an inspiration to everyone who knew them.

He ran his fingers through his rumpled hair. Was it possible that such a miracle could happen twice in the same family? If he married Susan to please his father, could they eventually fall in love with each other?

She was young and romantic and alone. She had a need to be a part of a family, and she'd probably already convinced herself that she was falling in love with him. There was a smoldering passion in her that responded to his caresses. It shouldn't be difficult to convince her to marry him.

But what about him? He put the photo back on the dresser and turned away. He loved his father, but was he prepared to make a sacrifice of this magnitude to give Vito the grandchild that was so vital to him? Marc desired Susan, but he didn't love her. Because he knew he couldn't have her in a casual relationship, she was a challenge now, but once he'd wedded and bedded her and gotten that out of his system, he'd be tied to a woman with whom he had nothing else in common.

He sat back down on the edge of the bed and dropped his head into his hands. He was caught in a trap of his own making. He wanted a woman like Susan for the mother of his children, but he preferred a sophisticated woman like Hilary as a lover and companion. He wanted a wife who had the best qualities of both Susan and Hilary, and such a person didn't exist. Those two women were opposites in every way. He was reaching for the impossible.

It was no wonder he couldn't sleep!

It was four days later, on Thursday, that Vito was released from the hospital to go home. Dr. Tornatori gave him strict instructions to rest and not try to work for at least a week, but the first place he headed when he got in the house was his office. After her initial protest, Susan realized that Vito's limited store of energy would give out fast, and then he'd have to stop and rest. She'd learned that nobody ever won an argument with Vito Donatello, but he could be persuaded if it was done subtly.

Ben stopped in to see his father on his way home from work. By then Vito had had a long nap and looked and acted happier than Susan had seen him since this latest setback.

Shortly after Ben left, Marco arrived. Susan hadn't seen him since Sunday, when he'd kissed her and run. Not a very flattering analogy, but very close to true. When he'd pulled her onto his lap and kissed her, she'd melted against him with no thought of the consequences. She'd never been so witless before with any man, but when Marc took her in his arms, all good reasons to resist fled, burned away by the heat that generated between them. She'd been thoroughly jolted when, after a few minutes, he'd put her aside, muttered something about having to go home and left.

He hadn't called or come by the apartment since. For that she was alternately grateful and disappointed. She appreciated his self-control since hers was so precarious, but perversely she almost hated him for arousing her and then casually walking away. Apparently he wanted both her and Hilary. She'd better stop behaving like a lovesick adolescent or be prepared for a lot of anguish if she ever let him make love to her.

She knew he'd visited his father in the hospital every night, but, since she had to take a bus clear across town to get there, she'd gone to see Vito in the afternoons while it was still daylight, so their paths hadn't crossed.

Now here he was looking at her with a longing that ignited an answering longing within her.

His voice belied the look, however, as he greeted her politely. "Hello, Susan. I'm sorry I wasn't able to pick Dad up at the hospital this morning, but I had an appointment that couldn't be put off. Thanks for doing it for me."

She felt like crying. "I was happy to do it," she said, forcing an unnatural lightness into her tone. "Walter drove us in the limousine."

Just then Mrs. Romano announced dinner, and Vito insisted that Marco eat with them. "I've been smelling spaghetti sauce all afternoon, and Mrs. Romano always cooks enough for the whole neighborhood."

Marc hesitated for a moment, then accepted. During the meal Marc and Vito talked business, and although Marc tried to include Susan several times, she kept her replies short. She'd intended to excuse herself and go to her room as soon as dinner was over, but while having cherry pie and coffee in the parlor, Vito suddenly changed the subject. "Marco, I have tickets for the Minnesota Symphony's Pops Concert tomorrow night. Leo insists I'm not to go out for a while, so why don't you take Susan?"

Susan cringed. What was Vito up to, anyway? Why didn't he just give the tickets to Marc and let him choose his own date? Vito made it sound as though he was bribing his son to take her. Thank heaven she had an excuse for not going. "Sorry, Papa Vito, but I can't possibly go tomorrow night. I have another date."

Marc raised one eyebrow. "Another date? With young Caldwell, I presume. Planning a wild night of beer and pizza at the corner pub?"

She wasn't going to let him bait her, and she smiled through clenched teeth. "Actually, no. We're having dinner at Murray's, then going to the Guthrie theater to see *The Merry Wives Of Windsor*. Afterward, we'll go to my apartment for coffee."

"Like hell you will," Marc grated. "You'll come back here after the show."

She'd figured that would shatter his smug superiority. "Where I spend the night is none of your business," she snapped. "I—"

"Enough, already," Vito interrupted. "Calm down, both of you. There's no problem. I'll have the concert tickets changed to Saturday night, but Marco's right." He turned to look at Susan. "I'd prefer that you live here full-time for a while, *bellezza*. The doctor said I must have someone with me at all times," he added piously, ignoring the fact that Mrs. Romano lived in. "You can bring your young man here for coffee."

That suited Susan just fine, since she'd had no intention of spending the night at her apartment. "Of course I'll stay here if you want me to, Papa Vito," she said, "but don't change the tickets. I'm sure Marc and Hilary can use them tomorrow night."

She knew it would be foolhardy to go out with Marc. The more she saw of him, the more she wanted to be with him. That was the main reason she'd accepted the date with Ryan. She'd never been as emotionally dependent on anyone as she was on the Donatello family, and it wasn't a dependency she welcomed. She should never have allowed it to happen, but since it had, the sooner she established her independence, the better.

Marc glared at her. "If you don't mind, Susan, I prefer to make my own dates. I'll pick you up here early on Saturday, and we'll have dinner before the concert."

She glared back. The nerve of him! He didn't even bother to ask, just told her. "I haven't said I'd go with you," she said petulantly and knew she was being childish.

"Oh, I'm sorry," he said, and his tone was sarcastic. "I didn't realize your date book was so full. Is there any chance you could squeeze me in on Saturday evening?"

Her smoldering temper exploded. "Not a snowball's chance in hell," she answered coldly, "nor at any time in the foreseeable future. Now, if you'll excuse me, I have letters to write." She turned and walked out of the room with as much dignity as she could muster, then ran up the stairs and into her bedroom.

She threw herself facedown on her bed, trembling with rage and frustration.

Why did she seem to invite Marc's taunts? What made him think he had only to snap his fingers and she'd do as he demanded?

She sniffled. Probably because that's what she'd been doing. All he had to do was pat her on the head, and she'd fall at his feet.

She should leave, go back to Philadelphia. If it weren't for Papa Vito, she would, but she couldn't leave him now. He was sick and he needed her, depended on her. He'd always been there when she needed him, and now was her only chance to repay him. It wasn't his fault that she and his arrogant son couldn't get along.

A shuddering sob shook her, but she refused to release the tears that burned her eyes.

Reluctantly she had to admit that she did bait Marc. She'd done it in the past, and she did it again tonight when she implied that she might be spending tomorrow night with Ryan. Up until then Marc had been friendly and polite, so why had she struck out at him? If she was going to tease the bull, she had no right to cry foul if it gored her.

Was Marc jealous of Ryan? Is that why he attacked her verbally every time Ryan was brought into the conversation?

No, that wasn't possible. Marc had Hilary; he didn't need Susan, so there was no need for him to be jealous. It was more likely that he just didn't like her and resented the fact that he was physically attracted to her.

A knock on the door startled her out of her introspection. She drew her knees up and curled into a ball on the bed. "Go away," she called and buried her face in the flower-print ruffled spread.

She didn't hear the door open, but when someone sat down on the side of the bed, she rolled over and looked up into Marc's somber eyes. He reached out hesitantly and stroked her cheek with his palm. "Susan, I'm sorry," he said, and there was genuine contrition in his tone.

His remorse, coupled with her anger, was more than she could handle, and the tears that had been fighting for release flowed unchecked down her cheeks. "I—I don't want you here," she sobbed.

He uttered a sharp cry of anguish as he lay down beside her and gathered her into his embrace. "Oh, God, sweetheart, I'm sorry, I'm sorry, I'm sorry." He rained kisses on her disheveled hair. "I didn't mean to hurt you. I never, ever meant to make you cry."

Now that she had started she couldn't stop, and she rubbed her face in his shoulder and sobbed. He held her close and stroked her and murmured words of endearment until the storm passed.

When she finally lay quietly in his arms, too emotionally spent to speak, he said, "My sweet little innocent, I'm not surprised that you don't want to hear my apology. I'm a jerk."

Susan took a deep ragged breath, and his arms tightened. "I have a vicious temper and sometimes strike back when I'm hurt, then regret it later, but that's no excuse."

Susan looked up into his troubled face. "Have I hurt you?" she asked and sobbed again.

He tenderly licked away the moisture still left at the corners of her tear-swollen eyes. "You don't even know, do you? I must seem like a real creep to you."

She shook her head, but he brushed her lips with his and continued, "I've got to be out of my mind to be thinking of you as anything but a little sister. I'm too old for you. Too experienced. Too selfish."

Again she shook her head, but he captured it with one hand and guided it back to his shoulder. "I don't know how to say this so you'll understand, but I've always been the one in control in my relationships with women. I've started them, and I've been the one who ended them."

He paused for a moment and then chuckled. "I'm sure that sounds heartless to you, but always before I've had the good sense to choose only women who understood the rules and were willing to play by them. We had a good time while it lasted, and were able to walk away with no more than minor bruises when it was over. I never promised more than I was willing to give."

"You make it sound like a game," she said against his shirt, "but you've never promised me anything."

"I know I haven't, but I've taken all the warmth and caring you've offered without ever returning anything but insults and heartache. I want so much from you, but I don't want to give anything of myself in return. I've had it all my own way for so long that I've gotten spoiled, and I don't like what I've become."

He stroked his fingers through her blond curls, then kissed her on the temple. Ordinarily his kisses excited her, but now she was so emotionally drained that they relaxed her instead, and she burrowed against him.

He continue to stroke her. "Please go to the symphony with me Saturday, *amore mia*. I want very much to take you, and I won't use the tickets unless you go with me."

He paused for a moment as though unsure how to proceed. "I promise to behave like a gentleman, although I can't blame you if you don't believe that. I'd like to take you to dinner at the Orion Room on the fiftieth floor of the IDS tower. If you haven't been there, you mustn't miss it. The view is absolutely spectacular."

He rubbed his cheek in the softness of her hair. "Please forgive me for being such a jerk, and say you'll go with me."

Susan felt so warm and relaxed, and well cared for that she'd have agreed to anything he asked of her. "I'd like to go with you," she murmured lovingly, "if you're sure you want to take me."

She felt him relax against her then, and he sighed softly and whispered, "I'm sure," just before she fell asleep.

The lighted dial on Susan's alarm clock told Marc it was 12:45. It was dark, but he had no trouble remembering where he was, or identifying the woman sleeping in the circle of his arms.

After Susan had fallen asleep, he'd stayed awake as long as he could in order to savor the sweet intimacy of their bodies entwined on the soft bed, but eventually he'd drifted off, too. He wasn't sure what had wakened him, but already his relaxed state was giving way to stirrings of a more urgent nature. He didn't want to put himself through that type of frustration and carefully eased away from her, then slid off the bed and quietly opened and closed the door as he left the bedroom.

He was grateful for the heavy carpeting that absorbed the sound of his footsteps in the hall and on the stairs, so he wasn't prepared to hear Vito's voice call to him from the den. Marc made a quick detour into the room to find his father sitting in his big leather chair, looking tired and rumpled. "Papa, what are you doing still up at this time of the night?"

Vito glared at his son. "I'm waiting for you to come out of Susanna's room so we can start making plans for the wedding." There was barely leashed fury in his tone.

"What wed—" Belatedly the implication hit him. "Oh, for heaven's sake, Papa, I didn't touch her."

Vito eyed him balefully. "Then what were you two doing up there for the past five hours?"

"We were sleeping." Marc knew that was an unfortunate choice of words the minute they were uttered.

"*Where* were you sleeping?"

"On—on the bed, but look—"

Vito's hands gripped the arms of the chair. "I'll telephone Father Giuseppe in the morning and arrange for a date when both he and the church are available."

Marc slapped his forehead with the heel of his palm. "Oh, for... Look, I know it sounds incriminating, but *nothing happened*! We slept. That's all."

"I'm sorry to hear that. As far as I know, you're the first impotent Donatello man in the history of the family."

"I'm not impotent!" Marc roared. "Dammit, Papa, listen to me and pay attention. Susan was upset. I'd hurt her, as you well know, and when I went up there, she was lying on the bed crying. I lay down beside her to apologize and try to comfort her. It took quite a while, but when she finally calmed down, she agreed to go to the pops concert with me. A few minutes later she fell asleep. I held her for a while, then I slept, too. I just woke up, but she's still sleeping like a baby."

Marc snapped his mouth shut and fervently wished he hadn't mentioned *baby*.

Vito continued to glare at him for a moment, then unclenched his hands and settled back more comfortably in the chair. "All right, Marco, because you're my son and I love you, I'll believe you, but we'd better have one thing understood between us. I've made no secret of my desire for you to marry Susanna, but seduction is an abomination I will not allow. She's my goddaughter, the daughter I'd like to have had. Her father trusted me to take care of her after he was no longer here to do so, and I take my obligation seriously. You'll be treated the same as any other man where she's concerned, and that includes no more 'just sleeping' with her." He grated a course oath. "At your age you should know how dangerous that can be."

Marco looked straight at his father. "I don't want her hurt any more than you do, but I've been behaving like a self-centered tyrant. Her tears had a devastating effect on me, and I had time to think as I lay there with her sleeping in my arms. I don't know how I feel about her. Desire, yes—but love? Probably not. If I loved her, I'd be begging her to marry me, and frankly, the idea doesn't appeal to me. I like my freedom too well, but the thought of her with Ryan Caldwell really shakes me up.''

He sat down in a wing chair. ''I've come to one decision, though. I'm going to break it off with Hilary. We were more or less coasting even before I met Susan, but I've been holding on to the relationship as a form of... protection. Protection against myself, and my ambivalent feelings for that tempting young *tesoro* of yours.''

Vito smiled. ''My 'treasure.' That's an apt description. Susan is a treasure and I cherish her. I expect you to do the same. Break off with Hilary, if that's what you want, but don't use Susan as you've used your other women. If you're going to court her, your intentions had better damn well be honorable.''

Mark parked the Ferrari in the visitors parking area of the basalt block condominium building just off the Nicolette Mall and got out to open the door for Hilary. She put her hand in his and smiled up at him as she gracefully exited the low car.

She had a lovely smile. For that matter, she was a beautiful woman, tall and slender and elegant. It was her strawberry-blond hair that had first attracted him, but it was her sharp intelligence and her sophisticated outlook that had kept him interested.

They walked to the entrance of the building and took the elevator to the fifth floor. Marc smiled at her as they stood in the lift waiting for it to stop. Until he'd picked her up earlier to take her to dinner, he hadn't seen her since the day of the store opening in Duluth. She looked different somehow. He'd finally decided it was the print silk dress she wore. It was softer, more feminine than the tailored gowns she usually preferred. The low vee neckline was trimmed with lace, and a band at the hips topped a pleated skirt. It made her look younger, more vulnerable...

He looked away as the door slid open and wished she'd worn one of her dress-for-success outfits that proclaimed her an independent business woman. It would have made his task a little easier.

They walked down the hall to her door, and Marc opened it with his key, then placed it on the small marble topped table behind the lamp and turned on the light. He knew she expected him to spend the night, and he wanted to get this over with as quickly and as painlessly as possible.

Hilary closed the door and put her arms around him. He held her as she drew his head down and kissed him. "Fix us a drink, love, while I slip into something more comfortable," she said huskily but with a touch of humor to acknowledge her cliché.

He felt a twinge of remorse for the pain he was about to cause her. Hilary had always been straight with him, and he owed her the dignity of a clean break. "Come into the living room with me first," he said as he stepped away from her. "I'd like to talk to you."

She looked at him questioningly but moved into the living room and made herself comfortable on the couch while he poured their drinks at the bar.

Marc felt like a heel as he handed her a martini and sat down in a chair facing her. This was the first time he'd broken off with a woman who didn't already suspect that it was coming, and he knew he was handling it badly. Usually they just drifted apart and then started going out with others. Never before had he broken up with one woman because he wanted another, and he silently cursed the day Susan Alessandro had walked into his well-ordered life. She'd caused him nothing but frustration and anxiety, but when he'd been forced to make a choice, Hilary was the one he was discarding.

Discard. What an ugly word. He felt a sharp stab of guilt but took a deep breath and prayed that he could do this gently.

She looked straight at him. "What did you want to talk about?"

Marc was the first to look away. "Hilary, we've both known from the beginning that this relationship wasn't going to lead to a long-term commitment, and I feel that I've monopolized enough of your time. You deserve more than I'm prepared to offer."

He moved restlessly in his chair and was aware of the beads of perspiration that had broken out on his forehead and upper lip. Damn, he sounded like the cad in a Victorian novel.

"Have I complained?" Hilary asked sharply.

He could see that she wasn't going to help him out a bit. Well, why should she? He deserved everything he was going through. "No. No, you haven't complained. You've given without ever asking for anything."

She set her glass on the coffee table. "Then why this sudden concern for my welfare? You'll pardon me for saying so, but it's not like you to be so noble."

Good, she was getting angry. If they could work up a blazing quarrel, it would be easier on both of them. "I've never pretended to be noble, or even nice. I don't want to hurt you, Hilary. You've made me happy during the time we've been together, and you're very special to me, but I feel that it's time for us to go our separate ways.''

Hilary stood up and faced him. Her tone was no longer calm. ''In other words, you've decided to cave in to your father's demand for a grandchild and marry his homeless waif.''

Marc's hand jerked, and he spilled part of his drink as he jumped out of his chair. ''How do you know about that?'' he demanded, his own anger building now.

For a moment Hilary paused, as though she'd said something she hadn't meant to, but then she gathered steam again. ''I overheard you and Ben talking about it one night at Vito's. I really thought you had more spunk than that, Marc. I'm sorry Vito is so sick, but that doesn't give him the right to insist that you live your life for him.''

''Now look—'' Marc said, but she wasn't finished.

''You really had me fooled,'' she said as she picked up her martini and drained half the glass. ''I thought you were a grown man with a mind of your own, but it turns out you're just an overgrown little boy who still jumps to obey when Papa speaks.''

Marc had gotten more than he'd bargained for in the way of a quarrel. Now he was thoroughly enraged. ''And I thought you were a mature woman who'd outgrown the habit of listening at keyholes,'' he snapped. ''My father's illness and anything pertaining to it are strictly family business, and it will stay that way. Do you understand, Hilary? If you mention this to *anybody*, I'll show you just how grown-up I really am.''

She winced and turned away. ''It's not necessary to threaten me, Marc,'' she said, and all the fight had gone out of her. "I thought you knew me better than to think I'd broadcast your private tragedy."

She started walking slowly toward the bedroom. "Please leave now."

He heard the bedroom door shut before he could gather his wits about him to protest.

Chapter Eight

Susan sighed as she repaired her lipstick in the ladies' lounge of the Orion Room. If she hadn't given in to the temptation to order the chocolate-fudge cheesecake from the dessert menu, she wouldn't feel so full. It had been worth it, though. She'd never tasted anything so delicious.

The whole meal had been a gourmet's delight, and the view...! Marc had said it was spectacular, but that didn't begin to describe it. It seemed to her that she could see the entire state of Minnesota through the glass wall.

She put the lipstick back into her beaded bag and left the lounge to meet Marc at the bank of elevators. The frank admiration in his brown eyes as he watched her approach made her heart palpitate. She'd been surprised earlier in the day when he'd called to ask her to wear the blue lawn dress she'd worn to her first dinner party at Vito's home. It delighted her that he remembered the gown, but she'd made a few modifications. She wore her hair swirling around her shoulders instead of tying it in the childish pony tails, and she'd opted for white pumps instead of the laced ballet slippers.

Marc smiled and tucked her hand in the crook of his arm as he led her into the elevator.

Outside the weather was still uncomfortably warm and sultry as they strolled up Nicolette Avenue toward Orchestra Hall. Marc had driven over to pick her up in his Ferrari, but Vito had insisted that they let Walter drive them downtown in the limousine to avoid the problem of parking. Marc had muttered but finally gave in. Since Orchestra Hall was within easy walking distance of the restaurant, they'd arranged for Walter to pick them up at the hall after the concert.

It was still a little early when they arrived at their destination, and Marc said, "Would you like to take a turn through the plaza before we go in?"

The plaza in front of the hall was terraced downward to a square pool and thick green lawns. Water flowing out of steel cylindrical pipes of various heights cascaded over concrete blocks in several stragegically placed waterfalls creating a cool, peaceful resting place in the heart of the busy city.

They walked down the steps and wandered through the park, then sat down on one of the small blocklike benches next to a low-spreading cedar under a huge old shade tree. "It's beautiful," Susan said softly. "So peaceful, and I love the continuous sound of rushing water."

Marc took her hand in his. "You're beautiful," he murmured and kissed her palm. "Thank you for wearing my favorite dress."

She stroked his smooth cheek with her fingers. "Thank you for remembering it. You look nice, too. I like the light blue jacket with the dark blue trousers, but you always look great, no matter what you wear."

His eyes darkened, and he moved her hand slightly to kiss the pads of her fingers. "Talk like that is apt to get you more than you bargained for, and right here in public, too." His voice was husky. "Maybe we'd better change the subject." He lowered their entwined hands to lay on her thigh with his on the bottom next to the sheer fabric of her skirt. "Did you enjoy the play at the Guthrie last night?"

She had trouble bringing her attention back to his words. "Oh, yes. Yes, I enjoyed it very much. I'd read about the innovative Tyrone Guthrie theater, of course, but that was the first time I'd ever been there."

"Would you like to go again? I think *Saint Joan* is playing soon. I can arrange for tickets."

Susan wanted desperately to go with Marc, but in spite of the fact that two nights ago they'd slept curled up together on her bed, he was still involved with Hilary. Susan supposed her code of ethics was outdated, but it was the one she'd been brought up by, and it suited her. "I—I don't think so, Marc," she said regretfully.

He looked at her thoughtfully. "Is it because of Hilary, Susan? If it is, you should know that she and I are no longer...involved." The sharp pain that clouded his eyes for a moment was unmistakable, but with a blink it was gone. "I'm free by your standards, as well as mine, and I'd like to spend more time with you."

Susan's eyes widened. "You've broken off with Hilary? But I thought . . . When did this happen?"

He squeezed her hand. "Last night. We had a talk and agreed that it was better if we went our separate ways. We won't be going out together anymore."

Susan felt odd. She should be wildly happy, but she couldn't help but wonder if this had been a mutual decision or...

She looked away from him. "Marc?" She cleared her throat and started again. "Did this sudden breakup have anything to do with me? Am I the reason you've thrown her over?"

Marc winced. "I didn't 'throw her over.' Our relationship had lost its luster before I ever met you. It had never been intended as a long-term commitment. Hilary's not a starry-eyed girl, honey. She's as old as I am, and she's been on her own for a long time. I admit that I was the one who suggested that we stop seeing each other. I also admit that my interest in you hastened the inevitable, but Hilary was agreeable."

Marc knew he was coloring the truth. Hilary had been hurt, and for that he was truly sorry, but telling Susan would only make her feel guilty. There was no need for that; he felt enough guilt for both of them.

Susan smiled. "In that case, I'd love to go to the theater with you."

For the next two weeks Marc and Susan saw each other nearly every day. Often they went out, but sometimes Marc would come to the house for dinner. Afterward they'd spend the evenings visiting with Vito, who finally seemed to be responding to the treatments and was steadily getting stronger and feeling better.

He still retired early, though, and whether they went out or stayed in, Susan could barely restrain her impatience until they were alone together in the small comfortable parlor and Marc took her in his arms. They fit together so perfectly, his angles into her curves, his lips against hers, his tongue playing erotic games with her mouth.

Now that he was no longer seeing Hilary, Susan felt free to relax and enjoy his embrace. He was a tender but experienced lover, and he knew where to touch her and kiss her. She was sure he enjoyed it, too, but he seemed to discourage her efforts to return the pleasure.

Not that he said or did anything overt, but when she touched him or kissed him in some of the places that she knew were sensitive, he would remove her hand, kiss it and place it on more neutral territory, or he'd move so that her kisses fell short of their mark. She wasn't sure whether it was intentional or just bad timing, but she reluctantly curbed her impulses and just followed where he led. He never stayed late, and not once had he tried to go all the way.

She wasn't sure whether she was grateful or disappointed.

Marco knew exactly how he felt. A few more sessions like the one he'd just torn himself away from, and his self-control was going to shatter. He shivered with frustration as he slowed the car when the light ahead turned red. It had been fifteen years since he'd had to restrain his desire for a woman, and it was driving him around the bend.

From the age of twenty he'd dated women who were mature enough to know what they wanted, and savvy enough to understand that sex didn't necessarily result in love, marriage and children, in that order.

Not that Susan was immature for her age. Actually she had a lot of good common sense, but she was also incredibly naive. He could have taken her anytime he'd wanted to this past two weeks, and, oh God, how he'd wanted to.

The light turned green, and his hand trembled as he shifted downward and stepped on the gas. Didn't she know what she was doing to him! Didn't she understand that a man could only be tempted so far before he took what he throbbed for, and to hell with the consequences?

No, she didn't, and that's what was driving him out of his mind. She trusted him! He could see it in the loving way she looked at him, in her uninhibited response to his preliminary lovemaking. Somewhere, she'd gotten the idea that honorable men never lost control of their baser urges. She honestly believed that he would never hurt her.

He almost missed his turn and took the corner with tires screeching. One thing was sure, he couldn't go on like this. He'd had such good intentions. He'd keep their physical encounters light. Just a few kisses and a little caressing at the end of each evening together until he'd weighed all the pros and cons of marrying her and giving Papa his hope for the future, a grandchild.

Idiot! He'd had enough experience kissing her before to know she was dynamite, so what made him think he could light the fuse but prevent the explosion?

If he were sensible, he'd ignore Vito's request, find another woman and leave Susan alone. However, he hadn't done a sensible thing since that first day when he'd followed her tantalizing little figure down the hospital corridor to his father's room.

He couldn't stay away from her, and when they were together, he couldn't keep his hands off her. Maybe it was love. He'd certainly never been this obsessed before.

On the other hand, if it was only heightened sexual attraction, was it enough to build a marriage around? Her naïveté was refreshing, but would he still feel the same way a year from now?

For the first time Marc envied those of his friends who considered marriage vows expendable. They married on a whim, or a dare, or in the throes of sexual frustration, then had no qualms about divorce if it didn't work out.

Such a casual attitude was reprehensible to Marco. Especially when a child was involved, and his only reason for considering marriage at this time was to father another generation of Donatellos. When that happened, he'd be a full-time, totally involved parent and husband with no intention of shirking his responsibilities.

He slowed the car and turned into the parking garage under his apartment building. This indecision was messing up his whole life, and it was time to put a stop to it. He'd talk to Susan, casually, of course. Find out her views on children, and if she would be agreeable to starting a family immediately after marriage.

If her goals were the same as his, he'd ask her to marry him. His initial refusal to grant his father's impassioned request haunted him, and anything was better than this vacillating.

Susan hummed along with the clock radio as she dressed for her date with Marc. They were going to the Guthrie Theater again, this time to see Bernard Shaw's masterpiece, *Saint Joan*. Susan was fascinated by the famous theater and its talented repertory company, which attracted world-renowned directors.

It had been raining most of the day, and the brisk breeze was chilly. She wore a long-sleeve silk dress in pastel shades of blue and coral, with a set-in waist and pleated bodice. Her only jewelry was tiny diamond earrings, a high-school graduation gift from her mother and stepfather.

A flash of lightning drew her to the window just as Marc's red car came into sight on the winding hilltop road and pulled up in the driveway. She hurriedly ran the brush through her shoulder-length hair one more time, then ran down the stairs to meet him as he came in the door.

He caught her in his arms and hugged her, and she threw her arms around his neck and kissed him eagerly. His initial response was as eager as hers, but, more quickly than she would have preferred, he drew away from her. "Careful, *puppida*," he said, "I'm all wet." He brushed at his tan custom-tailored raincoat. "We'll ruin that pretty dress. Is Dad in the den? I'd like to talk to him for a few minutes before we leave."

"Of course. He'd feel slighted if you didn't." She started to take his arm, then thought better of it and walked along beside him. Maybe he didn't like to have her hanging on him all the time.

In the den Vito was sitting in the leather chair, reading a stack of folders on his lap. He looked up and grinned. "Ah, Marco, glad you got here a little early. I've been reading the latest report from the midtown store. That was a stroke of genius on our part, putting a market down there. The city council's so hot to bring residents back into the innercity, but no one but us thought to provide a place for them to shop for groceries. The volume of business is well above what we'd projected.''

Susan stood back as Marc took the folder his father held out to him and scanned it. From then on she was forgotten as the two men discussed business. Finally she left and went to the closet to get her raincoat. The play started at eight o'clock, and if they didn't leave soon, they'd be late.

She buttoned the lightweight red double-breasted garment and fitted the matching wide-brimmed waterproof hat at a becoming angle on her head, but still Marc lingered. Her hurt feelings were rapidly turning to anger, and she marched back to the den.

The two men were still bent over the report, and when she spoke, her voice was sharper than she'd intended. ''Marc, if we don't leave right now, we might as well not bother. We'll be late as it is.''

Marc started guiltily and glanced at his watch. ''Oh, I'm sorry, sweetheart, I lost track of the time. Why didn't you say something sooner?''

She didn't bother to answer but turned and walked toward the front of the house with Marc hurrying to catch up.

During the drive he attempted to start a conversation, but it died for lack of encouragement as Susan seethed in the seat beside him. *Saint Joan* was a highly dramatic play, and coming in late would dilute some of its tension. If Marc had business to discuss with his father, why hadn't he arrived earlier or waited until the next day?

She felt slighted, but also uneasy. Did Marc really care for her, or was he just making do with her until another Hilary came along? Sometimes he seemed happy to be with her, but at other times he was preoccupied, as though he had something else on his mind.

It was unsettling because her feelings for him grew deeper every day, but if he were just passing the time between affairs, she was setting herself up for a stunning blow. She'd allowed herself to fall in love with this domineering man, but she had no idea how he felt about her.

The car came to a stop, and Susan realized that they were in the parking lot. The rain had slackened to a sprinkle, and she put her hand on the door to open it, but Marc grasped her by the shoulders and turned her to face him. "I'm not going to let you out of this car until you listen to my apology," he said and leaned over to brush her lips with his.

Her resentment melted, and she leaned against him. "I'm sorry, darling," he said. "I didn't mean to ignore you, or make us late. I know there are times when I'm an insensitive boor." He lifted her chin with his fingers to make her look at him. "I don't mean to be, and I'm working on improving, but that's no excuse for hurting you. Will you forgive me if I promise that it will never happen again?"

His soft brown eyes were filled with remorse, and she couldn't have remained angry if she'd wanted to. She reached up and cupped his head with her hands. "I forgive you," she said, and he lowered his mouth to hers in a long, heated kiss that left her aching for more.

Approximately three hours later, after an unrelenting buildup of tension throughout, the play reached its shattering climax, with live flames circling the martyred nineteen-year-old maid of Lorraine who was burned as a witch, and later venerated as a saint. The powerful scene left Susan in tears as the audience rose to its feet with thundering applause.

On the way home Susan and Marc discussed the play, and the unorthodox theater in which it was presented. "I enjoy the Guthrie," Susan commented. "Its arrangement is so different. I've never been in a theater before where the stage was the middle of the floor, and the audience sat in tiered seats around it. It's very impressive. Almost like being a part of the action."

"Yes, it is," Marc agreed and squeezed her hand. "We're very proud of the Guthrie here in Minneapolis, and the players are excellent. The actress who played the title role did a magnificent job."

"Yes, she did, and the role of Joan is a difficult one. She was such an obsessively dedicated woman. She had an impossible goal, and never deviated from it, even when to continue meant being burned at the stake." She shivered as her mind revived the haunting scene. "Not many people, men or women, are willing to go to such extremes to get what they want."

Marc brought her hand up and rubbed the back of it against his cheek. "Speaking of goals, what are yours, Susan? What do you want out of life?"

She paused for a moment. "I'm afraid I'm not as ambitious as Joan of Arc," she said hesitantly. "I enjoy the work I'm trained for, but what I really want is a husband and children. I guess that's not considered much of a goal anymore, and certainly I'd want to work again after the children no longer needed me full-time, but I'd want to be there for them when they're small."

Mark kissed her palm, then returned her hand to her lap as he used both of his to make a sharp turn. "And how soon do you plan on starting this family?"

Something in the tone of his voice made her glance at him. He sounded as if her answer were a matter of importance. "Well, I think it would be best to wait until I have the husband," she said lightly and chuckled.

He didn't laugh back. "I know it would," he said somewhat grimly. "I meant how soon after you're married? You're young: would you prefer to wait a few years before tying yourself down?"

He was apparently serious about this conversation. She thought for a moment, then said, "I think that would depend on how my husband felt. I'd be willing to have a baby whenever it came along, but some men don't want to start a family that quickly." She laughed nervously. "I don't think I have to make that decision right now, though, since I don't have a husband yet."

Just then they rounded the last bend and pulled into the driveway of the family home. Marc turned off the lights, but instead of opening the door to get out he turned toward Susan and pulled her into his arms.

She went willingly, her earlier irritation forgotten, and raised her face to his. He removed her hat and tossed it on the back seat. "I've been waiting hours for this," he murmured and covered her mouth with his own.

Oh, so had she. Her lips parted to allow the intimacy he sought, and she scooted her hips closer so that her body fit against his. She loved the feel of him, but tonight there was an impediment. She was wearing a raincoat. Marc had carried his from the theater to the car because the rain had stopped, but since the continuing night breeze was chilly, she'd put hers back on.

Now it was interfering with their closeness. His arms tightened around her as though he, too, resented the intrusion. When he broke off the kiss, he reached for the buttons and unfastened them, then repositioned his embrace inside the coat.

"That's better," he said and moved one hand up to cup her full breast. "Susan, about that husband..."

His fingers were circling the tip of her breast through her clothes, causing it to send ripples of pleasure in all directions. "What husband?" she whispered against his ear.

"The one you want to spend the rest of your life with," he said huskily. "Would you consider my application for the position?"

She'd been occupied nibbling on his earlobe, and it took a second for his words to register. When they did, she blinked and raised her head. "What?" Surely he hadn't said what she thought he did.

His hand continued to caress her breast while he kissed her throat. "I'm asking you to marry me," he said softly, "and let me father those children you're looking forward to."

She felt as if all the breath had been knocked out of her lungs, and her heart pounded with shock. She put her hands on either side of his head, and moved it away from all the lovely things he was doing to her neck. "You want to marry *me*?" Her voice was squeaky with surprise.

He smiled and kissed the tip of her nose. "Of course I want to marry you, *amore mia*. Why does that surprise you so? You're everything I've always wanted in a wife. You're sweet and loving and intelligent, and I want you so bad I can hardly stand it."

Rockets seemed to explode in her heart as the full impact of what he was saying finally penetrated her fog of disbelief. Marc wanted to marry her! It was impossible, incredible, wonderful!

She threw her arms around his neck and hugged him. "Oh, darling, are you sure? I love you so much, but I didn't think you'd ever really take me seriously."

For a moment they sat entwined in each other's arms without speaking, their hearts pounding in matching rhythm. Then Marc broke the silence. "Does that mean yes, you'll be my wife?" There was a quaver in his voice.

She licked her dry lips. "I'd be..." Her voice broke and she started again. "I'd be proud and honored to be your wife, Marc. I love you more than I can say."

He kissed her again, and it was familiar but with something added. The hunger and pleasure were there, but there was also a new tenderness, a blend of passion and reverence that told her better than words that she was his now and was to be treated with the respect due a beloved wife.

"I hope you're not planning on a long engagement," Marc said a few minutes later. "I don't think my self-control will last much longer."

She nuzzled his neck and felt him shiver. It gave her a sense of power to know he wanted her. "My mother always said you should get to know a man well before you marry him." She paused for effect. "Do you think I can get to know you by next weekend?"

He chuckled and blew in her ear. "Miss Alessandro, I do believe you're almost as anxious as I am."

"At least," she murmured as his mouth found hers again.

Susan's own tenuous hold on control evaporated as Marc's tongue plundered her open mouth, and his hand wandered from her breast to her waist, then across her stomach to settle on her thigh. Her blood raced through her veins as he slowly gathered her full skirt higher, inch by inch, until only her sheer stockings were between his palm and her bare leg.

She bent her knee and rested it on his thigh in an effort to get closer to his searching fingers, which had found the top of her bikini panty hose and began tugging it down.

They were both trembling when he suddenly broke off the kiss and pulled down her skirt. She uttered a cry of protest as he straightened and put her away from him. "My God," he groaned. "I can't stand any more of that. Come on, I'll walk you to the door."

Susan was throbbing in every nerve end, and she didn't want the night to end this way. "Marc," she said hesitantly, "if we're going to be married soon, what's wrong with... I mean, the commitment's been made..."

Marc was asking himself the same question. What the hell was the matter with him, anyway? He was in agony, and she was willing. All he had to do was start the car and drive her back downtown to his apartment. He'd have to bring her back before morning, or Vito would kill him before he could explain, but they'd have most of the night together, and then maybe he could think of something besides his driving need.

He put his arms around her again, but gently, and she snuggled against him, trusting and willing to give herself completely with no reservations.

Then he knew what was bothering him, holding him back from accepting her most precious gift.

"Cara mia," he said and stroked his fingers through her hair, "have you ever been with a man?"

She shook her head against his shoulder. "No, but..."

"I've never made love with a virgin, either, and much as I want you, I feel it would be almost brutish of me to take you before we've had our union blessed before God. I want our wedding night to be very, very special, and I'm willing to restrain myself until then. Just, please, have mercy and set the wedding date soon."

Susan was so deeply moved that it brought tears to her eyes. What a thoughtful and loving gesture. How many men would put themselves through that kind of frustration when they had a woman in their arms who would do anything they asked? She must be the luckiest woman in the whole world!

She raised her head and kissed him gently as a single tear made a path down her cheek. "I think you're the nicest man I've ever known, and I'll love you to the end of time."

Marc was totally captured by the completeness of her love and trust, but an uneasiness dimmed a little of the wonder. She was so open and honest about her feelings, and he knew he fell far short of the paragon she considered him.

It was a terrible responsibility to be loved so deeply by a vulnerable young woman, and he'd never forgive himself if he inadvertently trod on her new and untried feelings.

He kissed her quickly before he got caught up in the rapture again, then got out of the car and went around to give her his hand. "I'll come by early in the morning for breakfast," he told her, "and when Dad gets up, we'll give him our news together."

He unlocked the front door, then took her into his arms once more. "Good night, my darling," he said and kissed her. "Sleep well."

As he walked back to the car, he wondered if having a virgin bride was really going to be worth all the cold showers he was going to have to stand under between now and their wedding day.

By the time Vito came downstairs, Susan and Marc had finished the king-size breakfast Mrs. Romano prepared for them. Even though it was Saturday, he was dressed and ready to start the day. Susan was delighted with the way his health problems seemed to be fading. She'd been deeply concerned about him, but lately he'd been feeling so much better, and he was getting steadily stronger.

They both stood as he came into the dining room, and Susan gave him her usual enthusiastic good-morning kiss before they sat down again.

Vito looked at Marc as Mrs. Romano set a plate of corned-beef hash and poached eggs in front of him. "Are you here early, or didn't you go home last night?" There was a gathering storm in his eyes.

Marc grinned, and help up his hand. "I went home, Papa, I promise," he said, "but I came back early. Susan and I have news for you."

"Oh?" Vito raised one eyebrow. "Good news, I hope?"

"The best," Marc said happily. "Your little *figlioccia* has agreed to marry me, haven't you, *cara*." He reached out and put his hand over hers on the table.

Susan could feel the radiance of her smile as she nodded, temporarily unable to speak.

For a moment Vito looked blank, then his face split in a grin that lit up the whole room. "You're getting married! That makes me very, very happy!" He jumped up and grabbed them both in a bone-crunching embrace.

He kissed Susan and held her for a moment, then clapped his son on the shoulders and beamed. "From now on I'll forgive you anything, anything at all," he boomed at Marco. "Have you set a date? No need to shilly-shally; I'll call Father Giuseppe and get the ball rolling." He turned to Susan. "You were baptized Catholic, so there won't be any delays. Oh, and we'll have to send an announcement to the newspapers...."

His thoughts were tumbling over themselves as he kept up a running commentary and made notes in ink on the white linen napkins, while Marc and Susan kissed and laughed and kissed again.

"Papa, listen to me." Marc finally managed to capture his father's attention. "We've already talked to Father Giuseppe and arranged for a small family wedding in the chapel two weeks from today at ten o'clock in the morning."

"Two weeks." Vito sighed. "Ah, that's good, that's good. I was afraid Susanna would want a big wedding that would take months to arrange."

Susan laughed. "No way, Papa Vito. I can't wait to become an honest-to-goodness member of the Donatello family. Two weeks is a long enough engagement for me."

Vito reached out and took her small hand between his two big ones. "You've made me very, very happy, *mia figlia*. I've wanted so much to see Marco married before—" He stopped abruptly, and there were tears in his eyes.

Without quite knowing how she got there, Susan was out of her chair and kneeling beside Vito, with their arms around each other and her head pressed against his firm bulky chest. "Oh, Papa Vito, it's you who has made *me* happy." Her voice quavered with emotion. "I love Marco, and I'll be a good wife. I promise."

He bent and kissed the top of her head. "You'll never regret this, *cara*. I'll see to it that you'll never regret it, and you and Marco will have such beautiful *bambini* together."

She had her face buried in his chest, but she heard Marc clear his throat rather roughly and felt Vito tense. She lifted her head to intercept an inscrutable glance between father and son. A tiny chill ran down her spine, but it was gone immediately and she laughed. "Would you mind if we get married first before making plans for children?" she teased.

Gently he pushed her head back to his chest and again bent to kiss her hair. "Of course," he said, and his voice trembled slightly. "Forgive me. I'm getting to be an impatient old man. I love you, Susanna, and it's a great joy for me to welcome you even more securely into my family."

Chapter Nine

Susan had never been so happy. In the week since she and Marc had announced their engagement they'd been feted every day at luncheons, dinners and cocktail parties given by friends in their honor.

Although the wedding would be small, with just family and close friends in attendance, Vito had insisted on hosting a reception for several hundred guests the weekend after they returned from their two-week honeymoon in Hawaii. They'd agreed, but only on the condition that it be held in one of the hotels, and that Vito would let the hotel management make the arrangements and do all the work.

Marco was having a set of rings custom designed for her, so she didn't have a diamond to show off yet, but all she cared about was that the wedding ring arrive in time for the vows. Meanwhile, they'd sent the invitations by telegram because of the shortage of time, and since then it seemed that everyone in Minneapolis and

St. Paul wanted to entertain them with showers and prewedding parties.

On this beautiful Sunday afternoon Susan was getting ready for still another gathering, but this one was different. The host and hostess didn't yet know that Marco and Susan were getting married.

Marc's brother, Ben, and Carla had been vacationing in Europe for the past two weeks and couldn't readily be contacted, so Marc, Susan and Vito had decided it would be more fun to wait until they returned and then tell them. Vito had sent a telegram to the hotel in New York where they would be staying for a couple of days before they flew on home to Minneapolis and invited them to dinner on the night of their return. He received an answering wire asking that he, Marc and Susan have dinner with them at their house instead. "We have a surprise for you," was the last line.

Marc arrived a little early and held Susan away from him to look at her in her new turquoise cocktail gown that exactly matched her eyes. "You get more beautiful every day," he murmured and pulled her into his arms.

He kissed her, and for a moment nothing else existed except the two of them and the excitement that flared when they touched. Susan's only regret was that they'd been so busy that they'd had almost no time alone together. She yearned to curl up with him in the privacy of a locked room. If they lost control, so what? They loved each other, and the wedding was inevitable.

As Marc released her, his hand brushed her low-cut bodice and slipped inside to stroke her breast. "You little tease," he muttered huskily, "you wore this deliberately because you knew what it would do to me."

She grinned, unable to deny it.

He leaned down and nibbled at her warm bare flesh. "If you're not careful, I'm apt to ravish you right here on the floor."

His kiss started a pounding deep in her innermost being. "Is that a promise?" she whispered.

He straightened then. "Believe it," he growled and put his arm around her to lead her into the living room.

"Have you talked to Ben yet?" Susan asked after they'd seated themselves comfortably on the couch. "I assume their flight got in on time this afternoon."

"No, I haven't, and yes, it did. Ben called the office, but I was out. He left word that they're looking forward to seeing us tonight."

"I'm just as anxious to see them. What do you suppose their surprise is, Marc?"

He shrugged. "They probably brought back extravagant gifts and can't wait to give them to us." He smiled. "Carla's so openhearted and generous. I think she'd rather give gifts than receive them. Every time they go on a trip, she brings back something for everyone she knows."

Just then Vito came downstairs, and they prepared to leave.

Ben and Carla lived in a luxurious town house in the exclusive Kenwood district on the shore of the Lake of the Isles. It featured vaulted ceilings, a cozy loft that peered down into the expansive living room, and a large deck. A home that fit perfectly into their life-style.

Susan was struck immediately by the aura of excitement that enveloped the couple. They both looked marvelously tanned and relaxed after a week of visiting relatives in Italy, and another week spent on the French Riviera.

In typical exuberant Donatello style they all hugged and kissed each other. When they finally settled down with before-dinner drinks, Ben, who was standing in front of the ebony marble fireplace, raised his glass for silence. "I have an announcement," he said, when they all looked up expectantly.

Ben continued, his face shining with unconcealed joy. "Carla felt pretty rotten on the long flight from London to New York and couldn't keep any of her meals down, so when we got to the hotel in Manhattan, I asked them to get us a doctor."

Susan tensed. If Carla was ill, why was Ben so obviously pleased?

Vito spoke up before Ben could continue, and concern throbbed in his tone. "Carla, *dolcezza*, is something wrong with you?"

Carla grinned and shook her head, but it was Ben who answered. "Not at all, Papa. The doctor says she's pregnant! Can you believe it? After all these years we're finally going to have a baby!"

For a moment the room was silent in stunned amazement, then Vito jumped up and hugged his youngest son. "Benedetto, *mio figlio*, that's wonderful! Wonderful!"

There were tears in his eyes as he turned to Carla, who was now standing beside Ben. "Carla," he said in a voice tinged with awe. He took her in his arms and rocked her tenderly as the tears streamed down his cheeks.

By now Marc and Susan had crowded around, too, taking their turn hugging and congratulating the couple.

Susan's eyes were also misty with happiness. Every baby was a miracle, but this one would be a special blessing. Carla had told her of the grief and disappointment she and Ben had experienced because of their childlessness, and Susan knew that they had given up hope of ever having a family.

She was surprised, though, by the depth of Vito's reaction. She knew that he had a soft spot in his heart for children, and that he would welcome a grandchild, but she was unprepared for his emotional response to Ben's announcement.

Marc happily pounded Ben on the back, then got Carla away from Vito and kissed her gently as he spoke softly to her. Susan hugged Ben and rubbed her wet cheek against his equally damp one. She couldn't find words to express her joy that this nice couple were finally being granted their most fervent prayers, but she knew they understood.

Susan forgot about her own announcement as the dinner table conversation revolved around the baby, and later, news of the relatives Ben and Carla had visited in Italy. Vito beamed, and once in a while Susan caught him dabbing his eyes with his napkin. She'd never seen a man get this excited over an unexpected grandchild.

While she sat next to Marc, she slowly came to realize that he was quieter than the rest. Maybe he just couldn't get a word in edgewise.

She reached under the table and put her hand on his thigh. He looked at her and smiled, then picked up her hand and brought it to his lips. "I'm sorry, sweetheart," he said, for her ears alone, as the others laughed and talked. "I hadn't counted on something like this. Do you mind if we wait until everyone calms down a little before we tell Ben and Carla our news?"

Susan shook her head. "Of course not, darling. We couldn't get their attention now, anyway, and I wouldn't dream of trying to capture their spotlight. We'll have to tell them tonight, though, or they'll hear it from someone else."

"Of course we'll tell them tonight. We're not leaving here until we do, but it would be better to wait until they run down a little." He squeezed her hand and returned it to his thigh.

She loved Marc, and she loved his family. Surely it must be against the law to have so much happiness. It swelled and throbbed in her and heightened all her senses. Colors were brighter, food tasted better, and the blended fragrance of the flowers and the candles in the centerpiece was headier. She wondered if heaven could be any more glorious.

They had dessert and coffee in the living room, and after a while Carla and Susan excused themselves to clear the table. They stacked the dishes on two large trays and carried them into the kitchen. "Thanks for the help, Sue," Carla said, "but now it's just a matter of putting the food away and loading the dishwasher. You go on back and keep the men decent." She giggled. "They won't tell dirty stories in front of you."

Susan grinned. "I'd hate to spoil their adolescent fun, but if you're sure I'm not needed, I'll run upstairs and freshen up."

She went into the dining room and closed the door behind her. She could hear father and sons laughing in the living room as she crossed the floor to the stairway on the opposite wall.

In the dressing room off the master bedroom she made minor repairs to her makeup, then hurried to return to the others. It was time for Marc and her to tell

Ben and Carla about their engagement and coming wedding.

She stepped out onto the loft that jutted out over one end of the living room and could hear the muffled sound of water running and dishes being stacked in the dishwasher behind the closed kitchen door. Directly below her the men were sitting on the sofa, out of sight, and talking.

She'd turned toward the stairway when she heard one of them mention her name. Curious, she stopped and moved closer to the balustrade. She didn't intend to eavesdrop, but Ben's words froze her to the spot.

"...would have called you from New York, Marc, as soon as we found out Carla was pregnant, but she wouldn't let me. Wanted to tell all of you in person, but I was scared to death you might give in to Dad's plea for a grandchild and propose to Susan before I could get back to tell you it was no longer necessary, that you were off the hook, that I was providing the next generation to carry on the Donatello line, after all. Of course, I couldn't tell that to Carla, so we waited."

Susan gasped and stepped back. What on earth was Ben talking about? What did Vito have to do with Marc's proposal of marriage? Why did she feel like someone had dropped a rock in her stomach?

Marc spoke. "Ben, I—"

Ben continued without acknowledging the interruption. "You had no right to put that kind of pressure on Marc, Dad. He's entitled to choose his own wife the same as I did, and to have children when he wants them, not because you need grandchildren to assure the continuation of the family."

Susan felt dizzy and clutched at the railing. This wasn't happening. It was some kind of a nightmare, and she'd wake any minute.

"There's nothing wrong with arranged marriages." This time it was Vito's voice. "He'll never find a sweeter, more suitable wife than Susanna. She loves him, and she wants children. She's young, healthy and willing. What more can he want?"

Susan bit on her fist to keep from crying out with pain. No! Not Marco! Marc loved her. He wanted the marriage as much as she did. He'd never let anyone, not even his father, push him around, tell him how to live his life. He loved her! He did! He did!

"Ben! Dad! Shut up and listen to me, dammit," Marco thundered. "Ben, I've already asked Susan to marry me. We've been waiting until you got back to tell you. The wedding takes place this coming Saturday."

For a moment there was silence, then Susan heard a groan. "Oh, my God, Marco, I'm sorry," Ben said. "Is there any way you can get out of it?"

Susan swayed and would have lost her balance if she hadn't been clutching the railing with such force. She thought she'd known pain when her mother died, and again when her stepfather abandoned her, but it was nothing like this. She wasn't sure she could survive such heart-shattering agony.

Even more frightening, she didn't think she wanted to.

Before Marc could answer Ben, Carla came into the room. "Hey, you guys, hasn't Susan come down yet?"

Carla walked across the thick carpet to a chair by the fireplace and glanced up as she sat down. "Oh, there you are," she said as she spotted Susan hunched over and gripping the railing in the loft above. "What are you doing up there, Sue?'' A note of alarm crept into her voice. ''What's the matter? Are you all right?''

All three men jumped up at once and hit the stairs on the run.

''Susan! Oh, my God!''

''Son of a—!''

''Madre di Dios!''

The pain that looked out of Susan's eyes dimmed her vision and paralyzed her reflexes so that she could only stand there staring through a haze of anguish as the sound of pounding feet seemed to shake the floor.

Marc was the first to reach her. ''Susan! Oh, Lord, how long have you been here?''

He tried to clasp her in his arms, but she continued to stand with her hands clamped to the rail, frozen with shock, as the others crowded around her.

''Sue, I'm sorry! I had no idea...'' Ben was speaking.

''It's not what you think, Susanna,'' Vito said.

The voices, all talking at once and sounding frantic, seemed to vibrate off the walls and surround her, but she didn't attempt to sort out the words. She wished they'd all go away so she could crawl in a corner somewhere and hide.

''Susan, listen to me.'' Marc was trying to pry her fingers from the railing. ''Darling, let go and come downstairs with me so I can explain—''

''What in hell's going on here?'' Susan recognized Carla's voice and looked up to see her pushing the men aside as she strode toward her.

''What's the matter, honey?'' Carla said as she put her hand on Susan's rigid arm. ''What happened to upset you so?''

Maybe it was the fact that Carla was another woman, or possibly it was the bewilderment in her voice that told Susan she wasn't a participant in this despicable conspiracy, but something snapped inside her. She could feel her senses begin to function again, and the blood once more started flowing to her head and heart.

There was a lot of commotion going on around her, but it was only the voice of her thoughts that she heard.

She'd been made a fool of.

The three men of the Donatello family had coldbloodedly chosen her as the handmaiden to breed the next generation. They'd set her up for marriage to the eldest son. Not because Marco loved her, wanted her, needed her, but because for some reason known only to them, she fit the job description. They probably needed a sacrificial virgin, and she was the only one left in Minnesota.

Marc still had his arms around her as he tried to disengage her hold on the rail. His embrace was repulsive. "Let go of me," she said in a cold clear tone.

Carla's hand dropped, but Marc continued to hold her. "Susan, I know what you must be thinking, but—"

"I said, take your hands off me." She moved quickly to let go of the banister and shove him away from her.

She looked around and spotted Carla. "Carla, call a taxi. Tell them to hurry."

Carla nodded and hurried toward the bedroom.

"You're not going anywhere until we get this settled," Marc said and grabbed for her again.

She sidestepped him, and her voice was as icy as the look in her eyes. "Don't touch me. Don't ever touch me again." Her arctic gaze roamed over the three stricken men. "You disgust me, every one of you."

Vaguely she noticed that Vito was leaning heavily against the wall. He seemed to have shrunk and aged in the past few minutes. He looked old and ill. For a second she felt a stab of alarm, but it was quickly replaced with her building rage. If he was sick, it was probably because his carefully laid plans had just caved in on him, and Vito Donatello wasn't used to being thwarted.

Marc didn't look so good, either. His face was white, and there was anguish in his dark burning eyes. He, too, was obviously upset about the disintegration of their plans for a dynasty. Apparently in all the commotion he'd forgotten that Ben had finally sired the necessary heir.

"Sweetheart," Marc said in a raspy tone. "Please, let's all sit down and talk about this rationally. I'll stay away from you if that's what you want, but at least listen to me."

"Stop badgering her, Marco." It was Carla, who had reappeared beside Susan. "I don't know what's been going on, but I'm going to see that it doesn't go any further."

She touched Susan on the shoulder. "I called a taxi, and told them to get her *immediato*, but I'd really rather take you home."

"*I'll* take her home," Marc announced. "That's better, anyway. If we're alone, I can calm her down and make her understand."

"You can go to hell." The wrath in Susan's tone was chilling as she turned and walked to the stairway.

Carla caught up with her at the front door and handed Susan her stole and purse. "Susan," she said, "I haven't a clue as to what's upset you so."

"Ask your husband," Susan answered as she took the items. Then her voice softened. "Thanks, Carla. I'm so glad you weren't in on this, too."

The lights of an approaching car stopped in front of the town house, and Susan hurried down the walk toward it. The driver got out, but it was Marco who appeared from nowhere and opened the door for her. He gave the driver Vito's address and handed him a bill, then leaned down to speak to her through the open window. "We'll be right behind you, sweetheart," he said.

Susan rolled up the window and told the driver to step on it.

As they pulled away, she gave him the address of her apartment in the area of the university and told him to hurry.

The driver shrugged. "But the guy said—"

"It doesn't matter what the guy said," she gritted between clenched teeth, "I'm the passenger, and I want to go to the address I gave you. Now speed it up."

"Yes *ma'am*," the driver muttered and pressed down hard on the gas.

At the apartment Susan called to Mrs. Caldwell as she climbed the stairs and told the landlady not to admit anyone who came asking for her. She locked her door and began pacing around the two small rooms, too churned up to sit still.

How could they! How could three intelligent businessmen resort to such underhanded tactics? And why? Marco could have any woman he wanted, so why had they chosen one he *didn't* want to do the breeding honors? Why her? Ben's words still haunted her. *You're off the hook.... No longer necessary to propose to Susan.*

And that last, awful question: *Oh my God, Marco, is there any way you can get out of it?*

Susan shivered as humiliation washed over her, and she leaned against the wall and covered her flaming face with her hands. She wondered if they'd deliberately set out to demean her, or if they hadn't given a thought to her feelings one way or the other.

No wonder Marc had refused to make love to her. He didn't want to! Now that she thought back she realized that he'd never said he loved her. Not even when he'd asked her to marry him! She'd thought he was so noble for insisting they wait until they'd said their marriage vows when all the while he just plain hadn't wanted her. He apparently considered taking her to bed a duty he preferred to postpone as long as possible.

Susan was trembling now, and she wrapped her arms around herself and slowly sank to the floor where she huddled against the wall, her eyes closed and her mind racing out of control.

She'd been sitting in that position for some time when she heard a commotion downstairs, then the sound of someone taking the steps two at a time as Mrs. Caldwell's voice protested loudly.

"Susan!" It was Marco, and he banged on her door as he called. "Susan, let me in."

She just sat there, unable to respond as the banging continued.

"Sweetheart, I've got to talk to you. What are you doing here? Why didn't you go back home?"

She covered her ears with her palms, but Marco's bellow could be heard all over the house. "Susan, open this door! I'm not going away until you do."

She heard a siren in the distance before Marc drowned it out. "Susan, for heaven's sake at least answer me. Are you all right? Say something."

Again she heard the siren, louder this time, before Marc again outshouted it. "If you don't unlock this door, right now, I'm going to break it in. I'm not kidding, Susan. I'll give you till the count of three. One.... Two...."

It was as if she were a spectator, and the woman crouched on the floor was someone else. It didn't even occur to her to answer or try to quiet him down.

"Three!" Something hit the door with such force that it flew open, and Marc lunged in, stopping only inches from where she sat huddled against the wall with her hands still over her ears.

"Oh, Lord," he murmured as he looked down at her.

Susan heard more commotion downstairs as he leaned down and reached his hand out to her, and then there were two uniformed policemen and her landlady in the open doorway. The officers grabbed Marco from behind. "Okay, fella, what did you do to her?" one of them grated as he yanked Marc's hands behind him and snapped handcuffs on them, all in one movement.

Still in a detached state, Susan watched as they hauled Marc off to the other side of the room while he swore and argued with them. Imagine anyone brave enough to handcuff Marco Donatello. Vito would raise hell all the way to the governor's office.

One of the policemen came over and hunkered down beside her. He didn't touch her, but his gaze was thorough and clinical. "Are you all right, miss?"

She looked at him and nodded, for some reason unable to speak.

"Did he hurt you? Throw you around? Your landlady called and said he was creating a disturbance."

She shook her head and, with help from the officer, stood up. "We...we had a quarrel." Her voice was scratchy, and she cleared her throat. "He didn't touch me. I'm all right. Just tell him to go away and leave me alone."

She leaned against the door and watched as the policemen escorted Marc out of the room while he struggled and shouted at them all the way down the stairs. The front door opened and closed, and a few minutes later two cars drove away.

By Thursday Susan had received numerous phone calls that she didn't answer, several telegrams and special delivery letters that she tore up unopened, and armloads of flowers that she refused to accept from the delivery man. All from Marco.

What did Marco want of her, anyway? She'd made an unpleasant scene when she'd found out about his deception, but he was home free now, so why didn't he just stay out of her life? Did he get some kind of kick out of tormenting her?

She'd placated Mrs. Caldwell, discouraged Ryan from going after Marc and punching him out once he arrived home and learned what had happened, and had had time to snap out of her self-pity and think. She'd decided to go back to Philadelphia. It had been her home for seventeen years, and she knew it well. With her degree in business and her natural affinity for that line of work, she shouldn't have any trouble getting a job.

She'd saved enough money while living at Vito's home to pay for her flight back and keep her until she either started to work or could begin receiving unemployment. Susan was a survivor. She'd proven that before when things had gone wrong.

Maybe she'd even be lucky enough to stay all frozen up inside and would never have to feel the pain she knew was there just waiting to strike.

A knock on the door interrupted her packing, and she opened it to find Mrs. Caldwell standing in the hall. "Susan, I know you wanted me to tell anybody who came askin' for you that you're no longer here, but there's a taxi driver outside who gave me this envelope." She handed it to Susan. "Says it's from a Dr. Tornatori, and it's urgent."

Susan blanched. Leo. Vito's doctor. Her heart began to pound. Had Vito collapsed again?

She turned the envelope over and saw Dr. Tornatori's return address printed on it. There was no reason for him to get in touch with her unless...

Her hand shook as she tore it open, but then she paused. Vito Donatello was no longer any concern of hers. His backstage manipulations had nearly destroyed her, so why should she care whether or not he was sick?

"Go ahead and read it, girl," Mrs. Caldwell prompted. "The taxi man's waitin', and he says he's going to stay here till you do."

Slowly Susan pulled the sheet of notepaper out and unfolded it. It was brief.

Susan,
It's critically important that I talk to you about Vito's illness. I need your help. Stop being so damned stubborn and come to my office—now. The taxi will bring you.

Leo

She slumped against the doorjamb, and the pain she'd been dreading began seeping slowly through her body. Oh, please, no. She didn't want to feel it. She didn't want to care about Vito or any of the rest of his family. She just wanted to be left alone.

"Well, do you have an answer?" Mrs. Caldwell asked. "The man's meter is runnin'."

Susan gave the only answer she could. "Tell him to wait for me. I'll be down in five minutes."

Half an hour later she stood in front of Dr. Tornatori's office door. She'd quickly changed from jeans into the only dress she had at the apartment, a royal-blue cotton with a full skirt and hand embroidery at the neckline, but she hadn't bothered with makeup, and the brisk breeze had blown her hair into tangles. She straightened and reached for the knob. If she looked like a waif, she was sorry, but it couldn't be helped.

Susan gave her name to the receptionist and was immediately ushered back to the doctor's office. It was noon, and there were no patients waiting. When the door was opened, the stocky gray-haired physician rose and came around his desk. "Susan, thank God you came. After Marco told me the way they'd been treating you, I wasn't sure you would. Come, sit down."

He took her arm and turned her, and that's when she saw the man standing in front of the window. It was Marco.

Susan tensed, and her first impulse was to turn and run, but all she could do was stand there and gape. Even with the light behind him she could see that he looked drawn and haggard. His face was tinged with gray, and his eyes had a hollow, bruised look.

Her first thought was that Vito must indeed be ill. There was no other reason for his son to look so anguished.

Marc neither moved nor spoke. No matter what he said or did, it would be wrong. He'd been behaving like a bumbling idiot ever since Susan Alessandro had come into his life. He'd been too dense to understand how deeply he loved her until he'd carelessly blown his one chance to claim her as his beloved wife, to have and to hold forever.

A fresh onslaught of torment caused him to wince and clench his fists. She looked so...so fragile. The picture of her as he had last seen her, crouched on the floor, huddled against the wall and looking up at him with those huge pain-filled eyes, was almost more than he could bear.

Dear God, what had he done to her? Was he destined to live his remaining years in this unceasing purgatory? Would he ever be able to convince her that she was dearer to him than his own life?

She turned away from him, and he bit back a cry of despair.

Chapter Ten

Susan finally tore her gaze away from Marco and looked at the doctor. "Leo, why?" Her voice was raw. "I didn't expect you to betray me, too."

"I didn't betray you." He moved from behind his desk and put his arm around her, then led her to the couch and sat down beside her. "Marco insisted on being here, and I finally took pity on the poor jackass and agreed, but if you want him to leave, I'll happily throw him out. He doesn't deserve any consideration, if for no other reason than that he's a nincompoop."

Marco didn't react but stood silently watching them.

Susan was tempted to insist that he be evicted. She'd hoped to get out of town before he cornered her, but since she hadn't been that lucky, she realized that a confrontation was inevitable. "It doesn't matter," she said sadly. "Look, Leo, I was in the middle of packing when your summons arrived, and I'd like to get back to it. My flight leaves in the morning, so if there's nothing else . . ."

"You're leaving Minneapolis!" Marco finally spoke.

"There's nothing to keep me here." Her tone was bitter.

"But there is something else," Leo said. "I didn't ask you to come as a favor to Marco. It's Vito I'm concerned with."

Susan's stomach muscles clenched sickeningly. "You mean he really is ill?"

"I'm afraid so. I realize that you don't owe him a damn thing after the way he exploited you for his own selfish reasons, but I've known that bullheaded *italiano* for a long time. We come from the same town in Italy, and I'm convinced that he honestly thought he was making legitimate arrangements for a secure future for his goddaughter, as well as seeing to the continuation of the family line."

Susan shook her head and tried to speak, but Leo continued. "You have to understand that the men of my country have always taken care of their women, protected them, planned carefully for their future."

He grinned. "I got that knocked out of me when I married an American woman and had three fiercely independent daughters. He was simply acting in the same way that generations of Donatello men before him had. I don't say he was right, only that his motives were pure."

"That doesn't give him the right to go behind my back—"

"True," Leo interrupted, "and ordinarily I'd let him stew in his own mistakes, but Vito is also my patient, and that overrides my respect for your privacy."

"What's wrong with him?" Apprehension was thick in her tone.

"He has leukemia."

Susan's eyes widened with horror. "Leukemia? But that's—"

"It's a malignancy of the white blood cells and blood-forming organs, and it's often terminal."

Marc spoke. "Dammit, Leo, you don't have to be so brutal."

Dr. Tornatori glared at him. "You keep out of this, Marco. You and Vito have not been straight with Susan, yet you've allowed her to become more and more deeply involved emotionally. You then have the gall to wonder why she won't have anything more to do with either of you?"

He patted Susan's hand. "She's a lot smarter and stronger than you give her credit for, and it's time you stopped trying to 'protect' her and started telling her the truth."

Susan's head spun as she struggled with the shock and grief that overwhelmed her. She'd been right all along. Vito wasn't suffering from simple exhaustion: he had a severe and dreaded disease!

But why hadn't Marc told her? Several times she'd expressed her suspicion that Vito's illness was more serious than they'd admit, but he'd always denied it. Now this doctor was telling her he had leukemia!

She tried to speak, but there was something wrong with her vocal chords. Maybe it was just as well. She could feel the tears obstructing her throat and pressing against the back of her eyes.

Oh, God, why did she still care so much?

Someone shook her gently, and Dr. Tornatori spoke. "Susan, are you all right? Aren't you going to say something?"

She tried to swallow the knot in her throat. "Is he going to...will he...?" She couldn't say the hated word.

"Will he die?" Leo said it for her. "Yes, of course he will—we all do—but I can't predict whether or not his life span will be shortened by the disease. Vito is fifty-seven years old, and he has a chronic form of leukemia. People have been known to live for twenty or more years with it and lead normal lives."

The doctor took her cold hand in his. "Vito's a tough old bird, and he's responding well to the treatment we've been giving him. I'd be willing to bet that he'll outlive me, but not if he doesn't take care of himself. I'm worried about him, Susan. Since you left his home, he hasn't taken much interest in anything, not even the business. He's grieving, my dear. He realizes now how wrong he was. I'm asking you to let him tell you so. He needs your forgiveness."

"Oh, dear Lord!" The cry was wrenched from Susan as she bent forward and covered her face with her hands.

Even as the tears gushed down her cheeks and sobs shook her body, she was aware that Dr. Tornatori stood up and Marco took his place on the couch beside her. He pulled her into his arms and held her close while the storm of weeping convulsed her.

It didn't even occur to her to pull away from him. Instead she snuggled into his warm familiar embrace and let the tears flow as she mourned for the godfather she loved so dearly.

After a while she realized that the sobs weren't all hers, and she put her arms around Marc's neck and held him as his own tightly controlled grief gave way.

She lost all track of time, but eventually their sobs slackened and their tears dried up. It was only then that she was aware of Marc as a man, snuggled with her on the couch, and not just as another suffering human being offering and accepting comfort from intolerable pain.

She raised her head, and rubbed her wet cheek against his. "Oh, Marc," she said in a voice that got caught on a faltering sob. "Why didn't you tell me? I would have been your friend. We could have comforted each other and worked together to care for Vito."

She stroked her fingers through his thick hair. "If you and your father had come to me and told me what he wanted, and why, I might even have agreed to an arranged marriage in order to give him the grandchild he wanted."

Another sob shook her. "I just don't understand why you lied to me. Why you didn't trust me."

"Because I'm an obstinate muleheaded know-it-all jackass, just like Leo said." He kissed the indentation beneath her ear. "I was even too dim-witted to recognize how intensely I love you."

Involuntarily Susan jerked, then stiffened and pushed away from him. "Don't say that! Why can't you understand? I don't want to hear any more of your lies."

Marc reached for her again. "Susan, I'm not lying—"

She jumped to her feet, avoiding him and the words she was afraid to believe. "Where's Dr. Tornatori?" she asked as she looked around, then realized that he must have left some time ago. "Oh, never mind. I'm going to see Vito."

Marc caught her by the arm as she started out the door. "I'll take you," he said and matched his steps to hers.

Forty-five minutes later Marc unlocked the front door of his father's home and ushered Susan inside. "Papa's probably in his room," Marc said, "but we'll check down here first. He's spent most of his time just moping around, looking lost and lonely since you left. Seldom gets up before noon, and that's not like him."

"I don't understand," Susan said as they surveyed the empty living room and moved on to the den. "Why should he be depressed? Ben and Carla are giving him the grandchild he wanted. He doesn't need me anymore."

The den was also unoccupied, and Marc turned to look at her. "Do you honestly believe that the only thing he wanted you around for was to provide him with a grandchild? Think, Susan. When he invited you to come to Minneapolis and work for us, he had no idea he was sick. All the years he kept in touch with you long-distance he was in perfect health. He loves you. You've taken the place of the daughter he's always wanted. He may have gone about it all wrong, but he wanted to make sure you were taken care of if the illness couldn't be controlled."

Marc reached out and lifted her chin so that she looked into his eyes. "You and I will work out our differences later, but don't make Dad suffer any more than he already has for his poor judgment."

His gaze was unflinching, and she knew that what he said was the truth. Vito's meddling in their lives was wrong, but he'd done it with the best of intentions, and because of that she could forgive him. At the time he'd just learned how serious his illness was. He'd been still reeling from shock.

Actually, she was grateful that he'd thought of her at all. Most men with families of their own to worry about wouldn't have.

Before she could reassure Marc, Mrs. Romano came into the room. "Oh, excuse me, I didn't know anyone was...Susan!"

She rushed across the floor and clasped Susan in a motherly hug. "Ah, *bambina*, I'd almost given up hope that you'd come back. These Donatello men have been *impossibile*. Like great wounded bears who strike out at anyone and anything. Have you seen your *padrino* yet?"

Susan returned the hug. "Papa Vito? No, we were just looking for him. Do you know where he is?"

The housekeeper shook her head sadly. "He's in his room. He's seldom left it in the last few days. What happened on Sunday to upset everybody so? Nobody tells me anything."

"I'll tell you about it later," Susan promised. "Right now I must see Papa Vito."

Marco escorted her upstairs and knocked on Vito's bedroom door. "It's Marco, Papa. Are you awake?"

"Yes, yes, come in."

Vito was sitting in a worn leather chair with his head back and his eyes closed. His hands lay limply in his lap, and he was wearing faded slacks and a pullover sweater although the day was warm.

Susan was startled by his gray pallor and the listlessness she'd never seen in him before.

"I've brought someone to cheer you up," Marc said.

Vito frowned and opened his eyes. "I don't want..."

His gaze fell on Susan and he blinked, then blinked again. "Susanna!"

Susan ran to him and knelt by his chair as he leaned over and gathered her in his arms.

Marc backed out of the room and shut the door.

Downstairs he prowled around the spacious living room, trying to paste together some remnants of his shattered nervous system. Would Susan ever forgive him?

Probably not—why should she? He'd been so smug, self-assured and blind. So sure that he was the martyred hero who was giving up his cherished freedom to be the savior of the family name and provide his terminally ill father's last wish.

Hogwash! He'd been merely providing himself with an alibi for doing what he'd wanted to do all along: marry Susan. Why had he been too pigheaded to see it?

His life since Sunday night had been pure hell. With his usual arrogance, he hadn't fully realized how viciously he'd hurt her until he burst into her apartment and found her in a near-catatonic state.

He slammed his fist against the wall. If there was a shred of decency in him, he'd leave her alone, let her go back to Philadelphia and find a man who was worthy of her. A gentle man who wasn't too proud and egotistical to admit that he loved and needed her.

He slumped down in the nearest chair and put his head in his hands. He was so tired that it even seeped into his bones. He hadn't slept for more than a couple of hours at a time in days. Every time he closed his eyes, he saw those marvelous turquoise eyes of hers dulled with anguish and humiliation as she'd looked up at him from the floor on that awful night.

He lifted his head and sighed. He'd explained as best he could to the officers after they'd led him, handcuffed, from Susan's apartment, but the looks of contempt on their faces had filled him with self-loathing. He hadn't hit her, but what he had done to her was just as revolting.

When he'd identified himself to the policemen, they'd released him with a warning not to go near the house or Susan again unless invited. The disgust in their tone had told him plainer than words that they didn't believe his story but had no legal evidence on which to hold him.

Susan spent the better part of an hour closeted with Vito in his room, and as she walked down the staircase, she felt both relieved and grieved. Relieved to know that Papa Vito hadn't lied about his feelings for her. She knew now that he really did love her, and that his misguided efforts had been on her behalf as well as his own.

Her relief was tempered with grief, however. She'd worried about Vito's health since his first hospitalization, but at no time had she imagined that he was so dangerously ill. Dr. Tornatori's prognosis had been encouraging, but it was still only an educated guess.

As she stepped down onto the imported tile of the entryway, her intention was to retrieve her purse from the living room and leave as quickly as possible. She'd promised Papa Vito that she'd move back into the house, but not until tomorrow. She needed time alone to sort out her jumbled thoughts, and she didn't want to see Marco.

Although she could understand his motivation now, she still had conflicting emotions about the way he'd behaved. Her anger, hurt and humiliation were still open wounds that would take time to heal. She wondered if it wouldn't be better if they never did mend completely. She'd been very deeply in love with Marc, and it would be unbearable if she should discover that her love wasn't dead but only hiding until she could face it and deal with it.

Now that her fury had been defused, her strongest feeling when she thought of him was embarrassment. She'd been so naive and gullible. It hadn't even oc-cured to her that Marc would want to marry her for any other reason than that he loved her. That was probably why she'd never noticed that he hadn't said he did. How transparent she'd been.

Her high heels made a tapping sound on the tile as she crossed to the living room. The noise stopped when she stepped onto the Persian carpet and hurried to the chair where she'd tossed her purse when she first came in.

A voice behind her broke the silence. "Did you get everything straightened out with Dad?"

Marco! She whirled around to see him sitting in a dark leather chair in the far corner of the room. Darn, she'd hoped to get out of the house before... "Yes, I think so." She tried to smile but it didn't come off. "We had a long talk, and we both understand each other better now. I persuaded him to let me get him settled in bed before I left. He said he hasn't been sleeping well."

Marc ran his hand through his hair. "It's obvious that he's the man in this family with all the luck. I'd let you tuck me into bed, too. Anytime you wanted."

A wave of heat left her tingling. "Stop it, Marc!" She picked up her purse and clutched it to her. "It's no longer necessary to pretend with me. I understand bet-ter now why you thought it was earlier. Eventually I'll probably even be able to forgive you, but please don't humiliate me further by teasing me."

"Teasing you!" He jumped up and crossed the room to stand in front of her. "Teasing you is the furthest thing from my mind. I'm trying to tell you that I love you, not to mention how much I want and need you."

"Oh, for heaven's sake, Marc, knock it off." Anger, triggered by the way he could set her heart pounding even when she knew he was lying, made her tone harsh. "I admit I've been a fool, but no more. You don't have any feelings for me at all. You didn't even want me enough to take me to bed when you knew I was not only willing but eager."

Her cheeks flamed as she remembered how she'd practically thrown herself at him.

"Didn't want you!" He clutched her shoulders and shook her gently as he swore in both English and Italian. "Have you any idea what it does to a man to continually repress his sexual urges?"

She opened her mouth, but he glared at her. "Don't you dare deny that I was aroused by you. There was no way you could not have known what you were doing to me every time I touched you."

She closed her mouth and had to admit that he was right. She had known, and she'd loved the power that knowledge gave her. "All right," she said softly, "I'll admit that you wanted to make love to me, so why didn't you?"

"That was a mistake I'm not likely to repeat." He shoved his hands into his pockets and turned away. "It was *because* I loved you that I wanted to preserve your innocence until after the wedding. You were offering me your virginity, and that was precious to me. I meant it when I told you I didn't want to take it until we were committed to each other in the sight of God."

Susan's eyes widened, and she felt as though her bones were melting. "Oh, Marc." Her voice was little more than a whisper.

He turned back to her, and his expression was grim. "There are a lot of times when I'm not a very admirable person, Susan, but in this I was honestly trying to do what I felt was right. Every time I held you, kissed you and got almost to the point of no return, I'd remind myself that you'd waited all your life for me. I could wait a few more weeks for you."

He tossed his arms in the air. "The frustration damn near killed me, so don't tell me that I didn't want you!"

Susan had a wild desire to throw herself into his arms and forgive him anything, but she got a firm grip on her emotions. There were still too many other unexplained parts to Vito's detestable scheme. Just because Marc really had wanted her in bed didn't mean that he loved her. It only proved that he was male, and she was a desirable female.

Her knees were threatening to give way, and she sat down on the arm of the couch. "Thank you for clearing that up," she said without looking at him. "It does awful things to a woman's ego to think that the man she loves…uh, loved…didn't even want to make love with her."

He gestured widely. "Dammit, Susan, I—"

"I know," she said quickly. "I believe you wanted me, but love…? If you love me you would have told me so long ago, or at least when you proposed to me."

Marc sighed and reached out his hand to her. "Come and sit down with me. Let me start from the beginning and explain. It's all so complicated and messed up."

She ignored his proffered hand but rose and walked with him to the furniture grouping near the big window that looked out over the bronze, yellow, orange and purple of marigolds, zinnias and chrysanthemums in the colorful fall flower gardens. Summer was drawing to a close, and the long cold months of winter were rapidly approaching. She shivered and wondered if there would ever be another spring.

They sat down on the formal rose-striped satin couch. Susan moved far enough away from Marc that there was no danger of them accidentally touching. The moment was awkward, and she felt unsure and vulnerable. She didn't know where to look or what to do with her hands, and the questions she'd wanted to ask had been erased from her mind.

Marc finally rescued her. "You've lost parents, so maybe you can understand how traumatic it was for me to be told that Papa's illness would probably be terminal."

She noticed that he, too, avoided the word *death*, and a wave of sympathy for him washed over her. She nodded, unwilling to trust her voice.

"The day I met you had been a hellish one," he continued and went on to recount his horror on learning of his father's grave illness, and his shock at being told that Vito expected him to marry a woman he'd never met and produce a child, all in the space of a year.

The corners of Susan's mouth quirked. It would have been funny if it weren't so tragic. It didn't require much imagination to know how Marco would react to that!

He sat up straight and once again ran his fingers through his disheveled hair. "I was absolutely flabbergasted. I protested long and loud, but he assured me that you were the perfect wife for me and mother for his grandchildren. Can you blame me for resisting? It had nothing to do with you personally. It would have been the same no matter who the woman was. I love my father deeply and would have done anything else he asked to make his remaining years content, but I could not allow him to stage-manage my life for me."

Susan could no longer control her need to reach out to him, and she put her hand on his knee. "Of course I don't blame you for resisting," she said. "He had no right to demand such a thing of you."

He picked up her hand and kissed it, then held it in both of his. "By that evening when I met you, I was seething with resentment and guilt. To make matters worse, I was strongly attracted to you." He grimaced. "Hell, I think I fell in love with you before I even knew who you were. We'd come up together in the elevator, and by the time I'd followed you down the hall to Papa's room, I was captivated. If I hadn't been so damned obstinate, I'd have realized that he was right: you were the woman I'd been looking for. Instead I rejected the whole idea. I wasn't going to be coerced into marriage with anybody."

Again Susan felt the pain of humiliation. She pulled her hand away from him and clasped it with the other one in her lap. "But something happened to make you change your mind," she said bitterly. "Why did you suddenly decide to make the supreme sacrifice and ask me to marry you?"

Marc turned and cupped her shoulders with his hands. "Stop that, Susan." There was anger in his tone. "You aren't even trying to understand. I asked you to marry me because I didn't have any choice. I couldn't stay away from you, and when we were together, I was half-crazy with wanting you."

"That's not love," she grated, "that's lust."

"If that's all it was, I'd agree with you, but don't forget, I abstained." He grinned at his delicate choice of words. "Oh, God, how I abstained. I jogged and took cold showers until I felt like a muscle-bound prune. Then I'd have another encounter with you, and have to do it all over again."

He pulled her against him and put his arms around her. *"Mia amore,"* he murmured, "I'm too old for that adolescent game. I don't have to put myself through that kind of torture any more; I don't have the patience for flirting and teasing."

His voice had a mesmerizing effect, and his arms even more so. While Susan's mind told her not to surrender to either, her heart and body didn't pay the slightest attention. She put her hand to the side of his neck and could feel the pulse racing there.

"The first time I put you away from me while I still could, I realized that my happy bachelor existence was in big trouble. I told myself I'd done it because Papa would kill me if I seduced you, but even as I tried to believe it, I knew it was ridiculous. I hadn't let Vito intimidate me since I went away to college, but for that very reason I wouldn't admit that I was in love with you. That would mean he'd been right, that you really were the one woman in the world for me and I'd been too self-righteous to see it for myself."

He brushed the hair away from her neck and nibbled at her warm flesh. "I did all the things a man in love would do. I broke off with Hilary, courted you, asked you to marry me and even resisted the overwhelming need to make love to you until it was legal. Everything but tell you I loved you."

He moved his mouth to the firm line of her jaw and traced little kisses along it as he lowered his hand to stroke her breast. "It was just general cussedness that kept me from saying it. My pride wouldn't let me admit I'd been wrong. If I've lost you because of it... Oh, sweetheart, I don't think I can live without you."

His errant hand strayed lower and settled under her dress on her bare thigh, raising havoc with the throbbing nerve ends in her lower body. "I do love you, Susan. I've never been in love before, and I had trouble recognizing it, but I was happy and looking forward to claiming you as my wife. It didn't even occur to me that the original reason why I should marry was no longer valid until Ben mentioned it. The minute I realized that you'd heard Ben apologizing to me, I knew that Papa's plea for a grandchild had nothing to do with my desire to claim you. I'd asked you to spend your life with me because I couldn't face a future without you. Because I loved you so much that you'd already become a part of me, and even in that first instant I knew that losing you would be more than I could bear."

His voice throbbed with the effort he was making to convince her, and she could no longer doubt his sincerity. His hands and lips were lighting fires in her that threatened to explode.

She raised her head and cupped his face between her hands. "Are you sure?" she asked in a voice that shook with tension.

"Oh, yes." His mouth brushed hers. "These past few days have been a nightmare. Do you think I'd have been so desperate to see you and explain if I weren't sure?"

He gathered her closer and kissed her eyelids. "I want to marry you on Saturday, as planned. We have the rings and the marriage license, and everything is going ahead as ordered. All we have to do is show up."

Susan gasped and lowered her hands from his cheeks. "You mean you didn't cancel the church, or the caterers, or anything?"

He smiled and let his fingers explore the inside of her thigh. "Not a thing. I've considered abducting you by force if I can't get you to the church any other way."

He moved to put his hand into his pocket and brought out a small jeweler's case. He opened it and held it out to her.

Inside was a beautifully matched set of gold rings set with diamonds. He removed the one with the large square stone set in the center, then took her left hand in his. His soft brown eyes glowed with love as he raised her hand to his lips and kissed it. "I love you, Susan. I loved you when I first asked you to marry me, and I'll love you all the days of my life. Will you marry me and let me show you how much I need you?"

Susan blinked back tears of happiness. She no longer doubted Marc, and she knew that her love for him was as deep and abiding as it had always been. She turned her head and kissed him. "I love and need you, too," she said in a voice that trembled. "I want very much to marry you."

He slipped the ring on her finger, then cuddled her to him and sought her waiting mouth. She put her arms around his neck and gave herself up to the tender seduction of his tongue and his hands and his incoherent endearments.

It was quite a while before Susan realized that the couch they were sitting on was hard and uncomfortable. She put her fingers on Marc's chin to break off their kiss and draw in some badly needed air.

She touched his lips. "Marc, do you still want to wait until Saturday to make love with me?"

"No." His answer was firm and unequivocal. "But there's no reason why we can't be married this afternoon."

Her eyes widened as he continued. "As I said, we have the license and the rings. We could drive over to the church and have Father Giuseppe read the vows."

Susan hesitated, and he hastened to reassure her. "Nobody else need know, and we'll go ahead with the wedding as planned on Saturday. I'm not going to let you get away from me again. I'll recite the vows once a week for the rest of our lives, if that's what it takes to convince you of my love."

He grinned. "We'll spend the time between now and Saturday in bed, anyway, so we might as well make it legal."

Susan felt as though her heart would burst with all the joy that swelled within it. She pulled his head down and kissed the corners of his mouth. "It means a lot to you to have a virgin bride, doesn't it?" she murmured against his cheek.

He turned his face and sought her lips. "I'd never thought of it one way or the other, but yes, it is important to me that *you* be my virgin bride. I'm so honored to be the man you've been saving yourself for. I guess that sounds awfully pompous, but I intend to be your first and only lover. I want the experience to be special for you."

He kissed her with a tender restraint that underscored his words.

She stroked an errant lock of hair back from his forehead and smiled. "Then we'd better find that priest. I think we've delayed this wedding long enough."

"Amen to that," he said fervently and kissed her again.

*   *   *   *   *

Silhouette Romance

COMING NEXT MONTH

#520 ALOHA ALWAYS—Emilie Richards
Nicholas Chandler III was hiding from the world—and himself. It took a
lovely mermaid named Toby Fielding to prove to him that you couldn't
hide from love.

#521 SNOW BIRD—Lass Small
The Civil War had ended, but Bridget Taylor was one Yankee
J.R. Winsome was determined to capture. Would Bridget be able to escape
and fly back north or would she find the south—and a handsome Texan—
to her liking?

#522 LOVE 'N' MARRIAGE—Debbie Macomber
Steely-eyed Jonas Lockwood not only needed a secretary who could file
more than her fingernails—he needed a wife. Was Stephanie Coulter,
secretary extraordinaire, woman enough for the task?

#523 THE BEST DEFENSE—Madelyn Dohrn
Her new neighbor was perfect—handsome, considerate, charming. So
why was Ross Hensley entertaining an endless stream of women?
Nikki Andersen didn't want to find out, even if he was now acting smitten
with her. She'd heard of loving thy neighbor but this was ridiculous!

#524 GOLDEN BOY—Lucy Gordon
He'd been racing's "Golden Boy" until an accident plunged
Lance Hamilton into darkness—and Connie Denver's professional care.
Could Connie help him turn defeat into victory—as well as teach him to
love again?

#525 THE RAINBOW WAY—Laurey Bright
Reporter Alexia King was after a story—and only a story—but reclusive
Nathan Hazard thought she was after much more, and he was only too
willing to oblige. He'd waited a long time for Alexia, and wasn't about
to let her go—ever.

AVAILABLE THIS MONTH:

**#514 THE THINGS WE DO FOR
LOVE**
Glenda Sands

#515 TO CHOOSE A WIFE
Phyllis Halldorson

#516 A DANGEROUS PROPOSITION
Melodie Adams

#517 MAGGIE MINE
Karen Young

#518 THE BOY NEXT DOOR
Arlene James

#519 MR. LONELYHEARTS
Suzanne Forster

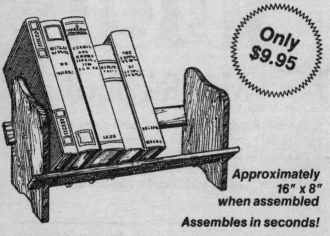

Sarah

MAURA SEGER

Sarah wanted desperately to escape the clutches of her cruel father.
Philip needed a mother for his son, a mistress for his plantation.
It was a marriage of convenience.
Then it happened. The love they had tried to deny suddenly became a
blissful reality... only to be challenged by life's hardships and brutal
misfortunes.
